A GANGSTER'S BBW OBSESSION 3
Written By: Mz. Lady P

Table of Contents

Chapter 1- Latasia
Chapter 2- Horse
Chapter 3- Draylon
Chapter 4- Horse
Chapter 5- Latasia
Chapter 6- Kateevah
Chapter 7- Draylon
Chapter 8- Belladonna
Chapter 9- Keizon
Chapter 10- Kateevah
Chapter 11- Tasia
Chapter 12-Keizon
Chapter 13- Belladonna
Chapter 14- Draylon
Chapter 15- Horse
Chapter 16- Kateevah

Letter From The Author

Dear Readers,

I want to thank you for making this series a Bestselling success. Your love and support does not go unnoticed. I love y'all real bad. I know that you love these characters and don't want the series to the end. Of course, they're powerful so you will see them again. Always keep in mind that there is a method to my madness. This time around I kept this book short, sweet, and straight to the point. I hope you all enjoy it.....

Chapter 1: Latasia

As I lay here blindfolded and strapped to the bed, I'm regretting the day I burned down *The Stable*. Horse vowed never to cheat again, which meant I needed to become his personal fuck toy. Just because I destroyed *The Stable* didn't mean that the sex demon was gone. If you ask me, it made him want to dominate me more. Don't get me wrong. I love the way he fucks me. However, sometimes it can be too much on my body. Horse is oblivious to the actual pain he inflicts on me.

The pleasure always overshadows the pain, so that's why I take this shit like a pro. I mean, what choice do I have? From the jump, I knew he was into this shit. I don't want him fucking other bitches, so I do what I have to do. At the same time, this nigga is putting miles on my pussy with the constant fucking he wants to do. Some days, we lay in bed all day naked and fucked like rabbits. Horse couldn't keep his hands off me. I loved it and hated it at the same time.

"What's taking you so long to cum on this dick?" he gritted and smacked my ass cheeks hard as fuck.

"Ahhhhhh!" I screamed as he stopped fucking me and starting eating my pussy.

My body shook as he feverishly sucked on my clit. With me being strapped down, I couldn't move much. I had just a little room to buck up against his face. Not long after, my pussy was raining everywhere.

"That's what the fuck I'm talking about! You better make that pussy talk to me!" The moment I stopped squirting, he put his dick back inside of me. Horse fucked me until I was pleading for him to stop.

When we were done, Horse unstrapped me and left me alone. That was another thing that was starting to bother me. He didn't make love to me anymore. It was more so straight fucking and punishing the pussy. The way he walked away afterward made me feel like a whore. I'm positive that's not his intention. I just think Horse is so detached from the softer side of sex.

Outside of that, life is so fucking good for us. I've never been happier. Horse goes above and beyond to make sure I want for nothing. The money was flowing abundantly, so I couldn't complain if I wanted to. My brother was happy, and Kateevah was happy, so I swear I really couldn't complain. Of course, we're still that toxic ass couple. We cuss, fuss, and do a whole lot of fucking when we make up.

Our son, Junior, will be a year old soon, but he looks like his ass is about to be two. My baby's gone be a big nigga just like his damn daddy. We shouldn't even be calling him Junior. We should be calling his ass Baby Horse. I love my fat daddy, though. He is everything I could have ever asked for.

"You good?" Horse asked as I climbed into bed next to him.

"Yes. I'm fine." I kissed him on the lips and laid my head on his chest. I loved the sound of his strong heartbeat. It was like a lullaby to me. This man was everything to me, and I couldn't imagine life without him. Deep down inside, I prayed that Horse knew I appreciated him.

↘ ↘ ↘ ↘ ↘↘

Uniquely Yours Hair Salon

"I should turn your ass around. When will you ever show up on time for your appointment?" I knew Kateevah's ass was going to be fussing at me.

"I'm sorry. It's Horse's fault. I told his ass I needed him to keep Junior while I got my hair done. When I woke up, his ass was gone, so I had to take him to Annalise. I'm sorry, friend. I swear I was trying to be on time."

"I just bet your ass was. Come over here and let me tame that shit." The moment I sat down in the chair, she started roughly combing through my shit.

"Hold on, hoe. I know you're mad at me but damn. Stop combing through my shit like that before I leave you a bad review."

"I'm sorry. I've got a lot on my mind, friend."

"What happened? We just talked last night, and everything was cool."

"I took another pregnancy test this morning, and it was negative. I just don't understand why I'm not getting pregnant."

"Maybe your ass isn't getting pregnant because you're actually trying. I think you all should just let God do his job. This is really starting to take a toll on you. I don't like how you sound. What does Draylon think?"

"He acts as if he's cool that we're not getting pregnant, but I know he wants me to have another baby. I haven't taken a birth control pill in eight months. Something is wrong, Tasia." Kateevah was damn near in tears, and it irritated the fuck out of me.

"Bitch if you don't get it together. I'll slap your ass. Stop crying. I promise you God is going to bless you and Draylon with more babies. You worry too damn much."

"You sound like my momma. I know that both of y'all are right, but you know how my anxiety gets when it comes down to giving Draylon what he wants."

I looked at my best friend, and it broke my heart. Not in a bad way. It's just that sometimes it seems like she loves Draylon too much. It's to the point where she puts herself on the back burner. Now, don't get me wrong. I love Draylon for my friend. He makes her happy, and she makes him happy as well. It's just that Kateevah has an unhealthy attachment to him. I know you hoes are judging me for what I'm saying. We all know me, and my man is toxic and unhealthy. The difference is we know we're fucked up. Kateevah or Draylon don't see it. As a matter of fact, they think they're the epitome of a great couple. I'm going to let them live, though.

"Trust me. Your ass is going to get pregnant. In the meantime, let's have some fun. We haven't been to the city to hang out in a minute. I lowkey miss our people," I brought up, changing the subject.

"Now you know Horse and Draylon would have a fit if we were in the city."

I rolled my eyes at Kateevah's scary ass. She never wants to just go against the grain. My girl done got too soft for me, so it's a must we go out and have some fun.

"Them niggas be in the city while they got us damn near locked up like prisoners. Hurry and do my hair. We're in the streets tonight. I promise we won't go anywhere where the niggas are off the chain. Honestly, I want to hear some good ass music and have some drinks. It's been a minute since we hung out, so let's get cute and chill."

"I know this shit is gone make Draylon mad, but you're right. Plus, Unique and DJ are spending the night with Annalise and Granny. You know they done moved in together."

"In a minute, I'm gone think they bumping pussies with they slick asses. I'm telling you. Thelma and Louise be on bullshit."

"I swear they stress me out, but at the same time, I'm happy they've been chill lately, not to mention helping with the kids."

"Yes, I love how they spoil my baby. However, I don't trust their parenting style. Granny is the reason Horse is the way that he is."

The moment the words left my mouth, he walked inside the shop. I smiled hard as fuck, looking at my baby walking toward me and counting money. Horse was dressed in a business suit, looking like a gangster and a gentleman.

"Hey, sis. How much does my baby's hair cost?"

"Two thousand dollars plus a tip!"

I fell out laughing. Kateevah knows damn well my hair doesn't cost that much.

"Here's five bands. That should cover the next hairdo. Aye, how long is this gone take?"

"Why?" I inquired.

"I was thinking we could catch a flight out and get married. It's time to make shit official," Horse answered.

Before I knew it, I had jumped out of the chair and into Horse's arms. He held me so tight.

"Are you serious, Horse?"

"Hell yeah. I've never been more serious about anything in my life."

"Well, nigga if you're serious, why in the hell are you not down on one knee? Where the fuck is my ring at?" If this nigga was really ready, he was half stepping with this proposal.

"Goddamn, Tasia. I'm not the nigga for all that shit. Are you marrying me or not?"

"Yeah, nigga, but I want a motherfucking rock on this finger when I say *I Do*. You hear me, Dayvion?"

"Yes, Latasia! I hear you, baby. Finish getting pretty and call me and let me know where you want to get married." Horse grabbed me by the throat and kissed me passionately before walking out of the shop.

"Oh my god, Tasia! I'm so happy for you. Come on, sit down. Let me slay your hair." Kateevah was so excited as she hugged me.

I sat back down in the chair and drifted into deep thought. The overthinking had been creeping in like crazy.

"I wonder why he all of a sudden wants to get married?"

"Now, don't you start with that bullshit. You were just getting on me. Now it's my turn to get on you. Horse wants to marry you because he loves you. I'm sure there is no ulterior motive. As a matter of fact, you two crazy motherfuckers were made for each other. Go and make that shit official, and then we will both be married to brothers at that. I swear this shit reminds me of the books I be reading. We really got us a hood fairytale. Don't worry. Horse wants you to be his wife, and that's all that matters. I love you, friend, and I'm so happy for you."

"You're right. I love you, too. I can't believe Horse really wants to get married, though. I'm going to embrace this shit, but I swear to God, I'm going to kill that motherfucker if he plays with me."

"I thought you said you weren't going to try to kill him anymore?" Kateevah laughed.

"That was when he was just my Demon Dick baby daddy. The rules have now changed since he's going to be my Demon Dick husband."

I was dead ass serious. Horse better really be ready for this marriage shit. Hell, I'm not even sure if I'm fully ready. All I know is he's the man I want to grow old with. As I've stated many times, I know we're the epitome of toxic. As much as I hate to admit it, the truth is that Horse has a serious sex addiction. Yes, I love that dick and all the pressure that comes with it. However, I'm not fully sure that he will never want to dominate bitches. Yeah, he hasn't been doing it since I burned *The Stable* down, but that doesn't mean that down the line, he won't get the urge to do it. Then again, for Horse to want to get married means he might just be. I'm always so negative about him and our relationship, so this time, I'm going to raise the white flag and marry this man. One thing for sure and two for certain, I know I'll regret it if I choose not to become Mrs. Dayvion Prince.

ꙮ ꙮ ꙮ ꙮ ꙮꙮ

My eyes rolled in the back of my head as Horse ate my pussy. We were having sex for the first time as husband and wife. I was so happy he was making love to me on our wedding night. Lord knows I didn't want him fucking the dog shit out of me tonight.

"Why are you not cumming for your husband?" Horse asked as he stopped eating my pussy.

I gasped when he slid his dick inside of me. A bitch couldn't even respond as he fucked me slowly. Not long after, I was squirting and cumming all over his dick.

"Fuckkkkk!" I moaned out as he smacked my clit feverishly with his dick.

The heaviness of his dick made the shit so intense. I was gripping the sheets hard as fuck as he made me squirt like crazy. *Why did this man have to be such a beast in the bedroom?*

"Damn, Mrs. Prince, that pussy wet-wet! Your ass is pregnant!" Horse declared.

The bliss immediately drained from my body. "No. I am not. My ass is on the Depo shot!" I disagreed.

I got up from the bed and went into the bathroom to take a shower. My juices were running down my legs with each step. Horse had lost his damn mind talking about I'm pregnant. I rebuke that shit in the name of Jesus Devontae Christ.

"Your pussy was wet just like that when you were pregnant with Junior. I'm telling you, Tasia. Your ass is pregnant! Trust me. I know. I've fucked plenty of pregnant bitches. The pussy feels amazing."

"Spare me the details." I rolled my eyes, irritated as fuck, because I didn't want to hear about him and other bitches, not to mention him trying to convince himself that I was pregnant. There was absolutely, positively no way I was pregnant.

Instead of getting an attitude, I decided just to focus on the fact that our crazy asses were married. I smiled big as hell, looking at my wedding ring. Horse had done his big one. I couldn't wait to blind these bitches with all this ice.

As he slid inside of the shower, I wrapped my arms around him and placed soft kisses on his neck. Without hesitation, I dropped to my knees and gave the nigga some of the best head I ever had, all the while thinking, would I ever be able to fully sexually satisfy him? That and the fact that this nigga swears I'm pregnant, which I know that I'm not.

Chapter 2: Kateevah

I cringed, looking at another negative pregnancy test. It was driving me crazy that I was not getting pregnant. I'm not even sure why this shit is bothering me so badly. All I know is that Draylon and I fuck damn near every day, sometimes twice a day, so a bitch should be pregnant by now. Still, my doctor said everything is fine, so I guess I should chill out. Draylon is a young, vibrant, healthy man. I'm sure his soldiers are still marching.

Besides worrying about not getting pregnant, life is so good for our little family. Having DJ living with us has been so good. He and Unique are thick as thieves. My baby is crazy about her big brother. In the last year, DJ has managed to adapt to life with his us. It took some time for him to get used to our rules, mainly because the shit Draya taught him was crazy as fuck. The bitch really trained him to kill on sight. I'm happy Draylon and Horse have been working hard to keep DJ's emotions under control.

Draylon is the proudest father ever these days. It was one thing for him to have Unique. However, having a namesake was everything to him. Draylon spends so much time with the kids that it's like I have three badass children running around the house. I'm happy he has found a way to balance fatherhood, being a husband, and running the Prince family. Sometimes I fall back and admire the boss ass nigga he is. I'm happy to admit I don't worry as much as I used to because he's home more. He doesn't keep long nights anymore or early mornings. Those times are dedicated to his family.

Hearing Draylon come into our bedroom, I quickly wrapped the negative pregnancy test up. For some reason, I didn't want to tell him it was negative again. Just thinking about how everything is so perfect makes me sad. I really want to give him another baby. Prior to finding out about DJ, he was hellbent on me giving him a son. However, now he has his namesake, so he's cool with me not getting pregnant. I can't say that to him because it would come off weird as fuck. Plus, it sounds a tad bit jealous, and I never want to come off that way. There is no way I would ever be jealous of a child.

When I walked out of the bathroom, Draylon was laid back on the bed with his eyes closed.

"Baby, are you okay?"

"Yeah, I just got a banging ass headache after this fucking meeting with the council." He blew out a frustrating sigh as he sat up.

"Is there anything I can do to make you feel better?" I placed a kiss on his lips as I stood in between his legs.

"Yeah, get dressed. I need you to attend a benefit dinner with me. An important associate of mine has invited us to dinner at their home."

"This is too last minute, Draylon. It takes me hours to get ready. I have to do my hair and makeup, not to mention find something to wear."

"It starts at eight o'clock, so that's four hours to get ready."

"That's not enough time. Just go without me," I huffed.

The way Draylon's face distorted let me know he was mad.

"Listen, I need my motherfucking wife standing beside me. This shit is getting old with you always declining to attend business functions. I want my wife in the room just like the other niggas do. You need to be dressed and ready to go by seven forty-five. I'm not taking them bitch ass excuses. Step the fuck up! You wanted a nigga to stay in the game, and this is what comes with that!"

"Okay, Draylon. I'll be ready."

The only reason I didn't go off was because he was right. I've been declining Draylon's requests to accompany him to important events for months. It wasn't that I didn't want to go. I just feel like I wouldn't fit into that world. Knowing him, he knows why I won't attend and putting the pressure on me to go. I've learned that when Draylon thinks I'm displaying insecure tendencies, he goes off on my ass so I can straighten the fuck up. I don't like how he goes about it because it hurts my soft-ass feelings, but a bitch can't do shit but respect it.

ⱴ ⱴ ⱴ ⱴ ⱴⱴ

The Peninsula Hotel Ballroom

I was thanking my lucky stars for deciding to put on the most elegant thing I had in the closet. My hair was in a sleek ponytail with two spirals hanging down in front of my face. My face was beat to the gods. I'm not going to lie. A bitch cleaned up nicely, but I felt so out of place. You could tell the niggas in the room had money and power. I smiled hard as fuck, watching my husband work the room. It was like the men were breaking their necks to shake his hand and acknowledge him. Draylon looked so fucking good in his Prada suit and shoes. If he weren't my husband already, I would be at his ass. I smiled as we locked eyes, and he walked over to me.

"You look beautiful," he complimented me and placed a kiss on my cheek.

"Thank you, handsome." I straightened his tie, followed by a kiss on the lips.

"Oh my god! Draylon Prince, is that you?" A beautiful mulatto looking woman walked over to where we were. It irritated me immediately. *Hoe, why is you over here?*

"Hey, Javanna. Long time no see. This is my wife, Kateevah. Baby, this is Javanna. We went to high school together."

"Nice to meet you." She and I shook hands. I could tell she really wasn't trying to exchange greetings with me. Her eyes were glued to Draylon. I relaxed, though. He let that bitch know off the rip who I was. At the same time, I'm no fool. They asses were more than classmates.

"How is the law firm?" he inquired. I wanted to ask him why the fuck he cared, but I played it cool.

"It's going great. Business would be better if the Prince family would retain me. Dayvion has been dodging my calls, too. Tell him he better call me. It was good seeing you. Let me get over here. I have to do a speech. It was nice meeting you, Keisha."

"It's Kateevah, bitch!" She had quickly rushed off, so I'm sure she didn't hear me. Draylon heard me loud and clear, though.

"Really, Kateevah?" He laughed.

"Nothing is funny about that bitch saying my name wrong on purpose. Don't think I'm a fool, Draylon. That bitch is more than just a classmate. She either fucked you before or wants Horse to do something weird to her ass. I'm going to fuck her up."

"Calm down, baby. I promise you there is nothing for you to worry about. Were you really going to fight in them high-ass heels?"

"I'll come up out of all this shit to whoop her ass. I have to use the ladies' room. I'll be right back." I gave him a quick peck and rushed off.

Once I found the bathroom, I quickly rushed inside. Lo and behold, that bitch was in there.

"How much are you paying him?"

"Excuse me?"

"How much are you paying that fine-ass man to be your husband? I'm not trying to be disrespectful or anything. It's just that a man like that rarely goes for fat girls. You women are the type that have to pay for the dick. Look at you and look around you. Sweetie, you don't belong with that man. I bet you paid a pretty penny for him!"

Without thinking, I blanked out and started fucking this bitch up. All I saw was all the bullying and constant ridicule growing up. She was about to get the brunt of all the anger I'd kept inside. Like, who in the fuck does this bitch think she is talking about she means no disrespect, all while disrespecting the fuck out of me?

Playing in my face was something I wasn't dealing with. This bitch had all of this mouth and couldn't fight. I didn't even feel like this was a fair fight. The hoe wasn't even a challenge. She made me mad not fighting back, so I grabbed her face and repeatedly rammed it into the mirror. The bitch looked like Ronnie from the movie *Player's Club* when Diamond whooped her ass but worse. I was covered in blood, and it didn't faze me. My ass didn't snap out of it until Draylon had basically snatched me out of the bathroom.

"Oh my god! Call the police!" some white bitch screamed.

"What the fuck, Kateevah?"

"Don't yank on me like that!"

Draylon continued to pull me away from the crowd and out of the hotel. Once we got a safe distance, he turned around and gripped the fuck out of my throat. The fury in his eyes was some shit I had never seen, and I've seen him angry as fuck.

"Shut the fuck up! Why would you go in there and do that? I distinctly told you the type of event this was. I'm one of the biggest niggas in the fucking room. How in the fuck do you think it looks that my bitch in here fighting like a ghetto hood rat? Get the fuck in the car and don't say shit!"

If I wasn't so fucking scared to speak, I might have cursed Draylon the fuck out. He had a right to be mad because Draylon was right. It wasn't a good look. Still, he should have asked me what happened before popping off. I got into the car and slammed it hard as fuck.

"Aye Kateevah! Pipe the fuck down, aight!"

"Don't yell at me, Draylon! I am not your fucking child. I've told you that numerous times!"

"Are you fucking slow, Kateevah? Do you see how fucking angry I am? I'm telling you to shut the fuck up for your own fucking good!"

"What the fuck you gone do if I don't shut up?" I seethed.

My ass was getting beside myself, but I didn't care. I'm fed up with how this nigga be handling me. I'm tired of just being quiet to appease him and keep him happy. This man is talking to me so fucking recklessly, and I'm over it.

"Keep talking that tough shit! I'm going to show you better than I can tell you," he warned.

I waved Draylon's ass off and stared out of the passenger side window. No more words were spoken between either of us the entire ride. My feelings couldn't even be hurt due to me being so angry. I hated I let that bitch make me lose my cool. I hate I embarrassed my husband, but at the same time, I don't give a fuck.

↘ ↘ ↘ ↘ ↘↘

It didn't take long before we pulled up to the house. I didn't hesitate coming up out of my dress. I had blood all over the place. Thank God the kids weren't here. I could hear Draylon yelling on the phone. I quickly hopped into the shower and scrubbed the fuck out of my body. Although I had been strong and stood my ground, my feelings were extremely hurt. Draylon never checked on me, nor did he ever ask me why I was fighting that bitch. The nigga called me a ghetto hood rat, and that shit got me livid. The angrier I became, the more I cried.

After showering, I dried off and quickly dressed before grabbing an overnight bag and placing some clothes inside. After grabbing some other necessities, I headed down the stairs. When I made it down to the bottom, Draylon was standing there.

"Running again, huh?"

"I'm not running, nigga! I'm walking my ghetto hood rat ass out of this motherfucker and away from you!" I fumed.

I tried to walk around Draylon, but he yanked me back and squeezed the fuck out of my face. With each word, he gripped harder.

"Aye, Kateevah, check this shit out! Watch your motherfucking mouth when you're talking to me! Who the fuck do you think you're playing with? Your behavior and your mouth are out of fucking control. We've had this discussion before. Ain't no fucking leaving, so you might as well take your ass back upstairs and unpack that fucking bag. This shit here is until the casket drops. You and I both know I don't have any qualms about killing a motherfucker! Now, what are you going to do?" he grilled.

Tears streamed down my face, and I was shaking out of fear. "I'm going to go back upstairs!" I cried.

The sound of the doorbell ringing made both of us jump. He let my face go and walked over to answer the door. Seeing that it was the police, I quickly wiped my face.

"Can I help you, officers?"

"Sorry to bother you, Mr. Prince. However, we have a complaint that Mrs. Prince brutally attacked Javanna Jewel, and she wants to press charges. I'm sorry, but we have to arrest her."

"You motherfuckers aren't putting any handcuffs on my fucking wife. I'll bring her down to the station myself with our lawyer."

"Nah, it's cool," I interjected, walking over to them and holding my hands out so they could put the cuffs on me.

This wasn't even about me being guilty of whooping that bitch's ass. This was about me getting the fuck out of this house with Draylon. These fucking police officers probably saved my fucking life. For all I know, his ass was going to cut me up, too. Fuck that. I'd rather go to jail.

↘ ↘ ↘ ↘ ↘↘

The Next Day

I was happy as hell that Latasia was the one who bonded me out of jail. Lord knows I didn't want it to be Draylon or my mother. I was not in the mood to talk to either of them. My momma hadn't done anything. I just didn't want to hear her mouth about who Draylon was. I heard that shit enough from him. Lord knows I didn't want to hear anything he had to say.

"Are you good, friend?"

"Yeah, I'm good. Happy as fuck to be out of there. Thanks for coming to get me."

"You already know I was coming to get you. Now why in the hell did you beat the fuck out of her?"

"I don't want to talk about it, Tasia."

"Bitch, I don't care what you don't want to talk about. Usually, I'm the one who gets reprimanded for my behavior. Now it's my turn to get on your ass. We've been friends for a long time, and you never really fought unless provoked. You disfigured that bitch for life. I heard Draylon telling Horse that the bitch is going to need plastic surgery. He is so pissed, friend. That's why I need to know what that bitch said to you."

My emotions got the best of me, so I pulled my hoody up to cover my face. I swear I didn't want to cry about this shit because I didn't do shit wrong.

"The bitch is a lawyer who went to school with Draylon and Horse. From the moment the bitch started talking to Draylon, I knew they had fucked before. I swear to God, Tasia, I wasn't acting jealous even though you know how I feel about that nigga and other bitches."

"And you're not wrong if you were jealous! Keep going." Tasia flamed up a blunt as I continued to tell the story.

"I had to go to the bathroom, and when I walked inside, she was standing at the sink. That bitch had the audacity to ask me how much I paid for Draylon to marry me. She basically said I'm too fat to be with a man like him. Without saying the words, the bitch started going on and on about how I didn't fit into his world, so I showed the bitch the world I really come from and beat the fuck out of her. That bitch had all that smart-ass shit to say and didn't even fight back. In that moment, all the teasing and bullying I endured in grammar school came to me. I blanked the fucked out on her ass. It felt like I was trying to kill her. Before I knew it, Draylon was dragging me out of the place. Not once did he ask me what happened. He was more concerned about how I looked in front of his business associates. That nigga told my ass I was acting like a ghetto hood rat. He was yelling and chastising me like a kid."

"Don't cry, friend. You know how that nigga gets when he's angry. Draylon means no harm. You know when he calms down, he's going to be all over your ass and spoiling you rotten. As far as that bitch goes, she had it coming for the shit she said. You didn't do shit wrong but defend yourself, so don't be feeling all bad and shit. You need to go home and tell him why you did that," Tasia advised.

"I can't go home to him." At this point, I had completely fallen apart. The thought of going home with him freaked me the fuck out. All I could think of was the way he threatened me.

Tasia quickly pulled over and hugged me.

"Calm down, friend. You have to go home. Unique and DJ are there waiting for you. Friend, go home and look that nigga in his face. Let him know why you whooped that bitch's ass. The only thing he can do is accept that shit or not. Either way, bitch, you better go in there and stand on business behind your fucking respect. Kateevah, you know how we are with each other, so I'm gone keep this shit real with you. The problem is that you spend every day trying to make Draylon happy and forget about yourself too much. You allow him to run the show so much. I'm not saying you got to be a disobedient bitch like me. I'm just saying stand up to that nigga. That's your motherfucking husband, not just the father of your daughter. Let's not forget how you're currently raising his fucking son. I've watched how much you've evolved into such a wonderful mother and wife, so you deserve more respect from Draylon. However, the only way you're going to get that respect is if you put your fucking foot down. Stop crying and stand up to his ass," Tasia finished before she flamed up the blunt and pulled back onto the expressway.

I sat in the passenger seat and took in everything Tasia had said. She was right. I needed to go home and stand on what the fuck I did. I wished the kids weren't home. I was not really trying to argue with Draylon in front of them. Fuck it. I was going home and dealing with whatever the nigga was about to throw at me.

"Do you think we fit in with them?"

"The question is, do they fit in with us? We're the motherfucking prize. Fuck these uppity ass motherfuckers! Them niggas should be happy as fuck that they have some of the baddest BBWs rocking their last name. These hoes mad 'cause some plus-sized Barbies snatched up some rich-ass gangsters. Fuck them, friend! You better whoop a bitch every time she comes at you wrong. Go inside that house and stand your fucking ground. You are Mrs. Draylon Prince and deserve respect from him and everybody else."

"Thanks, friend. I needed that."

Before I knew it, I had leaned over and hugged Tasia. Leave it to my best friend to put me in my place. I don't even know where I would be without her sometimes. The bitch is batshit crazy, but I love the fuck out of her.

ﻥ ﻥ ﻥ ﻥ ﻥﻥ

About thirty minutes later, I entered the house and cringed at Draylon sitting in the living room as if he were waiting for me. Instead of saying anything to him, I headed upstairs to check on the kids. I peeked in at Unique and saw that she was knocked out, so I placed a kiss on her forehead before heading to check on DJ.

"Hey, Ma, you good?" Shocked wasn't the word I felt at hearing DJ call me Ma. My heart melted when he jumped up and hugged me. We had built a rapport but never really showed affection like that.

"Yes, I am. Are you okay?"

"Yeah, I'm straight. I'm happy you got out of jail. I thought you were going to leave me, too."

"Come over here and let me talk to you for a minute." I grabbed DJ's hand, and we sat down on his bed.

"I want you to know that I will never leave you. I promised your dad that I would help him raise you. Son, you have my word that I'm going to be your mother until God calls me home. I love you, DJ!"

"I love you too, Ma."

We engaged in another hug, and it warmed the fuck out of my heart. It was like all the negative emotions I was just feeling had subsided. Kids know they have a way of making everything better.

After sitting in that dirty ass cell, all I wanted to do was take a bath and go to bed. A bitch was exhausted as fuck. I'm aware that a conversation is much needed with Draylon, but that shit is going to have to wait until tomorrow.

Chapter 3: Draylon

The last thing I wanted to do was be mad at my wife. However, that dinner wasn't the time or the place for her to be fighting. It doesn't matter what the reason was. Of course, I know it had to be a valid reason. Kateevah doesn't bother anybody, so I'm sure she didn't start the shit. However, she finished it. Kateevah fucked Javanna up, and now the bitch is pressing fucking charges. It was bad enough Kateevah had pissed me off talking shit. Willingly, allowing handcuffs to be put on her has me livid. I was never going to let them pigs escort my wife out of our home.

A nigga couldn't rest until she was out of jail, but now that she's home, I can lay the fuck down. I'm already knowing my wife is pissed off at me, so I'm not even about to address the shit. I'm sure she's too tired to speak on it as well.

As I headed up to talk to her, I stopped hearing her and DJ talking. I've always loved their bond. From the moment I brought him home to officially live with us, Kateevah has stepped in to take care of him. Hearing him call her Ma made me feel so good. The way she talked to him had me choked up for a minute. I could feel the love in her voice. As a man, it makes me happy that my wife accepts the son I never knew I had. Kateevah is top fucking tier all the way around, which is why I spazzed out on her like that. No matter the circumstances, she was supposed to hold her composure. Now, it would be different if Javanna hit her first. However, I know for a fact that didn't happen because she was scary as fuck in high school.

My phone vibrated in my pocket, pulling me from my thoughts. Looking at the screen, I saw that it was a text from Granny.

Gangsta Granny: *Is Kateevah okay?*

Me: *Yeah, she's good.*

Gangsta Granny: *Good. We're on our way over to talk to her.*

Me: *Not tonight. She just got out, so I'm sure the last thing she wants to do is talk. Come over in the morning and make us breakfast.*

Gangsta Granny: *Okay. Take it easy on my girl. You know Kateevah don't fuck with nobody. I'm pissed off, Draylon.*

I stopped responding because she would keep texting. A nigga wasn't in the mood to speak on the shit, either. My mother and grandmother have been driving me crazy since they found out what happened. I've yet to hear from Belladonna, but I'm already knowing she is going to have some choice words for my ass.

"You good?"

"Yeah," Kateevah replied and swiftly walked past me. I followed her as she walked inside of our bedroom.

"Look, I'm sure you don't want to talk."

"I definitely don't. All I want to do is take a shower and lay down." She lowkey slammed the bathroom door in my face.

That was my cue to fall back. I'll give her the space she obviously wants. Tomorrow is another day, and we definitely will have a much-needed talk. Her ass has a case now, and she needs to understand the seriousness of it. I have some connections, so my wife will be straight. However, I know the bitch Javanna is going to be on some bullshit.

↘ ↘ ↘ ↘ ↘↘

Waking up and seeing that Kateevah was gone lowkey pissed me off. I really wanted to have a conversation with her before I headed out. She's not answering the phone for me either. I swear my wife really wanted that other nigga inside of me to come out on her ass.

"Good morning, son," my mother greeted the moment I walked into the kitchen. As promised, she and Granny were at the house. My son and my daughter were sitting at the table eating breakfast.

"Good morning." I placed a kiss on both of their cheeks.

"Kateevah had to rush to the salon. She forgot she had appointments this morning," my mother stated.

"We need to talk in the other room," Granny interjected and gestured for me to follow her. One could only wonder what this old lady wanted. Seeing my mother following us only added to my curiosity.

"What's good? I need to get over to the shop to talk to Kateevah."

"What are you going to do about this Javanna situation? You know she and her family have close ties to the state attorney. They are definitely going to press charges on Kateevah."

"I have it under control, Granny! I'm already ten steps ahead of you." I assured.

"Are you sure, Draylon? We've had problems with the Jewel family in the past. Them motherfuckers play dirty!" my mother stated with concern on her face, which blew the fuck out of me. She didn't have a thing to worry about.

"I got this shit handled, Ma. I'm telling y'all I do.'

"Promise me that you'll keep us in the loop about things."

"I promise, Granny! Let me get out of here. I need to go talk to Kateevah before I have this sit-down with Javanna's people."

I hurried up and left out of the living room. A nigga needed to get away from Thelma and Louise. They were definitely going to keep asking me questions and talking about keeping them in the loop. My goal is to keep their old asses so far out of the loop. They won't know anything.

ↆ ↆ ↆ ↆ ↆↆ

My anger rose with each step as I walked toward Kateevah's booth. The fact that she was cutting some nigga hair had me livid. He was smiling like a motherfucker as they conversed. The shit had me ready to kill this nigga, right now. Lucky for him, I left my gun in the car.

"Let me talk to you for a minute!"

" I'll be done in like ten minutes."

"Wait your turn like everybody else."

"This is my husband, Smooth. He's not here for an appointment."

"My bad. I didn't mean any disrespect, my boy."

"I'm not no fucking boy, and you did disrespect me. I'll holla at you later about that, though."

"That's enough, Draylon!" Kateevah put the clippers down and walked toward her office.

I was definitely on her fucking heels. It was one thing for the nigga to disrespect me, but her doing the shit had me livid.

"What the fuck you doing cutting some nigga hair?"

"Let me go, Draylon. I'm a hairstylist who just happens to be a licensed barber. I cut niggas hair too."

"Nah, that's the last nigga hair you'll ever cut!"

"No! This is my life and my career. You can't just do that!"

"Are you slow or something? Or is it that you just don't give a fuck these days?" I had Kateevah gripped by the face and squeezed as tight as I could.

"I don't give a fuck! Let me go! Stop it, Draylon."

"I'll stop when you stop fucking playing with me. You know motherfucking well that I would never approve of you cutting another man's hair. Make that the last nigga hair you cut."

"And if I don't?" she challenged.

Kateevah was really trying hard to make me take it there. I let her face go but made sure to stay in her personal space.

"Oh, I see. You need flash cards or examples of what happens if you don't."

"What? You gone kill me, too?"

I quickly took a step back from her. Hearing Kateevah say that hurt me. I would never kill her. Yeah, I know I played that card when I was angry. However, the look on her face shows me that she really thinks that I would. Honestly, it had rendered me speechless.

Instead of responding to her, I walked out of her office and left the shop. I made sure to make a mental note of the nigga who disrespected me. I guarantee he'll see me again behind the disrespect. In the meantime, I'm going to fall back on Kateevah with everything that has happened. I'll handle shit behind the scenes my way. Obviously, I'm coming at her wrong and too strong. My baby thinks I would actually kill her. I could see it in her eyes, and that felt fucked up.

↘ ↘ ↘ ↘ ↘↘

Jewel Residence

"Well, if it isn't Draylon Prince. Once again, my daughter has gotten herself into trouble behind you."

I held in my laugh because this woman still hated me. She

loved to blame everybody else for the shit her daughter got herself into. The whole time Javanna has always been with the shits. If she knew the amount of drugs Javanna sold for us back in the day, she would lose her mind.

"Hello, Mrs. Jewel. Nice to see you again."

"My daughter's beautiful face requires plastic surgery, so my husband and I expect the Prince family to foot that bill. Please don't upset her. She is extremely upset about being attacked. This is just a suggestion, but you need to get that wife of yours some therapy. She can't go around attacking women in jealous rages. Javanna is in her old room resting. I'm sure you remember where it is," Mrs. Jewel finished.

I was glad her ass walked away because I was in no mood for her shit. She's delusional as fuck if she thinks her daughter has the power to make my wife jealous.

"Can I come in?" I asked as I knocked on the door.

"Yeah, it's open."

When I stepped inside, I observed Javanna sitting up in bed. She had a long bandage going down the side of her face. Kateevah had really fucked her up.

"Listen. I'm sorry your face got fucked up. I'll pay for whatever it costs to fix it."

"I can pay for my own fucking surgery. Your wife is going to jail, and I'm going to make her pay for what she did to me.

"One thing I know about my wife is that she doesn't start shit with nobody. Cut the bullshit. This is me, Javanna. When we fucked in high school, you stayed fucking with people and getting beat the fuck up. Now keep the shit real. What the fuck did you do?"

"Let's just say your wife has no self-control. I admit I might have said some shit she didn't like, but at the same time, she didn't have to attack me like that."

"You can't tell someone how to react when you do shit to them. Look, what can I do to keep you from pressing charges? My wife needs to be out of jail so that she can take care of our children. I'm willing to pay whatever. Just give me a number."

"Draylon, you, of all people, know that I have my own fucking money. This isn't about money. It's the principle. Plus, I don't want your money. I want something else. If you give it to me, I won't pursue charges against your wife."

I had a feeling I was going to regret asking her what that might be.

"What do you want?"

"I want you to get me pregnant. My clock is ticking, and I'm ready to be a mother. I don't want to get pregnant by a deadbeat ass nigga who won't take care of their responsibilities. Draylon, you're a good man, and I'm sure you're a great dad. I want my child to have a good man for a father."

"I am married. There is no way I can give you a seed. Do you know how fucking crazy you sound? There is plenty of niggas out here who are good fathers. My suggestion is that you hit the fucking pavement and find him. I'm not that nigga, Javanna, so you might as well give me a number so that I can get the fuck out of here. I'm not with this weird shit." Yeah, this bitch had definitely lost her mind.

"I don't want your money, so prepare to get your bitch a good-ass lawyer. Bye, Draylon."

"This is not a game you want to play with me," I gritted and walked out.

Javanna was about to put her and her family in a situation she couldn't get them out of. I don't know why motherfuckers just didn't take the fucking bread and go. They go through all the bullshit emotions, only to get murked in the end. The last thing I wanted to do was kill Javanna. However, behind my wife, I'd make that bitch and her people a distant memory.

↘ ↘ ↘ ↘ ↘↘

Prince Properties

"What's good, bro?" Horse spoke as he stepped inside of my office.

"Shit, trying to send the rest of these checks out. I need to hire someone immediately. This shit here was Draya's job. I hate not being more hands-on with this shit. Going through all of this paperwork and invoices is giving me a fucking headache."

"Bro, you need to let Ma and Granny handle that shit."

I looked at this nigga like he had two heads. The last thing I'm trying to do is have their asses hands-on with anything. They ask too many questions and make moves without my permission. They both know I'm the head of the family and capable of holding shit down. However, they still question my decisions.

"I'm trying to keep them from the day-to-day operations. Both of their asses are too busy."

"Maybe that's the problem. They have nothing to do. I'm telling you, big bro. Granny and Ma are good as fuck at keeping the books. You must have forgotten who kept the shit in order before Draya started."

"I'll think about it because this shit ain't it."

"So, what the fuck happened when you went to talk to Javanna?" Horse asked as he fired up a blunt.

"That bitch has lost her mind. She said the only way she'll drop the charges is if I get her pregnant."

Horse bussed out laughing so hard he choked off the weed smoke. I should have known his ass would think this shit was funny.

"I see she's still crazy as fuck behind your ass."

"Nigga, this shit isn't funny. Kateevah would kill my ass if she even knew I went to talk to the bitch. Bro, she fucked Javanna up. Her ass has to have plastic surgery. She's laying up acting like Kateevah was jealous, so that's why she fought her. I still don't know what really happened."

"So, you don't know why Kateevah beat her ass?"

"Nah, I never got a chance to ask. Honestly, I went off seeing her fighting. Then we got home and argued, and shortly after, the fucking police came and arrested her."

A knock on my office door stopped me from talking.

"I'm sorry to bother you, Mr. Prince. This package just arrived in the mail for you."

"Thanks, Anita." I grabbed the box from her and sat it down on the desk. Once she left and closed the door, I inspected the package. It didn't look right.

"What, bro?" Horse stood up and looked at it suspiciously as well.

"You hear that?" I asked him.

I gently opened the box, and my eyes bulged out of my head. It was a fucking bomb with the countdown of three minutes left.

"I know that ain't what the fuck I think it is!" Horse gritted.

"We got to get out of here now!" I yelled, and we both rushed out of the office.

Even though it had three minutes left, it went off the moment we got out of the office. We made it out just in time. The force sent us flying in all different directions. As I was laid out with my ears ringing like crazy. My mind wondered about who in the fuck had the balls to try to kill me.

Chapter 4: Horse

"Be still, Horse. I have to change this damn dressing so that it won't get infected." Tasia fussed.

That damn explosion had fucked my leg up.

"That shit hurts. I think you're hurting me on fucking purpose."

"Nigga, please! I thought you liked pain." She laughed.

"Ain't shit funny. Go get my momma for real."

"Boy, fuck you and your momma."

"Really Tasia? Why are you saying fuck my momma?"

"I was just playing. You know I love your momma." She laughed and kissed me on the lips.

I swear she plays too fucking much these days, which I love. Still, it's better than her being mad at a nigga and calling me "Demon Dick".

"You play too much. Hand me the blunt out of the ashtray."

"You need to stop all of that smoking so that you can heal."

"Ever since we got married, you've been acting like you run shit."

"And do! I'm about to be running your ass for the rest of your life. Here. I'm about to go see what Kateevah is doing. Do you need me to do anything else?"

"Hell yeah. You need to do this dick when you come back."

"I got you." Tasia kissed me on the lips and walked out of the bedroom.

I laid my head back against the headboard in deep thought. A nigga's leg needed to hurry and heal. Both Draylon and I were out of commission for about a good two weeks. We need to get down to the bottom of where the fuck this hit came from. The only problem with that is the shit could have come from anywhere.

At times like this, I miss Draya. We would have been out and about patrolling and snatching motherfuckers up. Just thinking about her still chokes me up. We were close as fuck. I just wish she would have talked to me before siding with our father. They really did a good job of fucking shit up. For all we know, this shit could stem from something they did. It doesn't even matter because we're definitely going to find out and murk whoever sent the bomb.

↘ ↘ ↘ ↘ ↘↘

One Week Later

"I'm really not understanding why we can't just stay at our house," Tasia fussed as she packed clothes. I was trying to tune her out and chill with my son.

"Because it's safer for all of us to be in one place. Stop complaining and pack. The car service will be here in an hour."

I focused back on my son and tickled him. It's crazy how I never imagined being a father or a husband. Now that I am, a nigga has to do whatever I have to do to protect them both, which is why I'm getting them out of harm's way. If a motherfucker had the audacity to try us at Prince properties, they have no qualms about hitting us where we lay our heads. We're pretty ducked off from the city, so I'm sure niggas don't know our location. At the same time, you can never be too sure.

As Tasia continued to pack, I observed her phone going off.

"I swear I'm about to block La- La!"

"Why?"

"Because her ass has been acting very fucking weird. I haven't heard from her in months. I'm not in the mood for that wishy-washy shit with her."

"You and La-La are crazier than a motherfucker. Don't block her. That shit is not cool."

"You team La-La or something?"

"Baby, you know I'm team Tasia. I just don't think it's right to block your OG. Let's change the subject. I'm not trying to be on your bad side. A nigga's trying to fuck something later." She shook her head and walked back into the closet.

I needed to holla at Keizon about La-La. Her ass abruptly left town and hadn't been answering Tasia's calls. I can tell it hurt her feelings because they had become much closer. Nothing La-La does surprises me. However, it's weird that she up and left the way she did, especially since I had given her a house on the Prince property, which was something I hadn't divulged to

Keizon or Tasia. La-La was happy as hell and took the house without question, yet suddenly, she moved out of state with no explanation. Something was not right about that. Still, I couldn't really focus on that right now. There were more pressing issues at hand that needed to be dealt with.

Make no mistake, though. I'm going to find out why she bounced on my wife. I'm not okay with her feelings being hurt like this. I accepted La-La into our home so that they could mend their relationship, not to mention spending time with her grandson. Extending an olive branch and giving her a home was a gift of gratitude, so it was pretty fucked up how she flaked on Latasia and Junior.

"Horse, you need to stay off of that leg!"

"I have to get up and walk around on it. Honestly, it doesn't even hurt as much. Plus, I can't just be sitting around all day every fucking day, Tasia. In case you forgot, some niggas tried to take us the fuck out!" Yelling caused me to trip, which made me hurt my leg.

"See! Look at you! Sit down before you hurt yourself!"

"I'm good!" I limped out of the bedroom and to the kitchen.

The sound of the doorbell made me head over to answer. I knew it was more than likely the car service, so I quickly opened the door, seeing that it was Keizon.

"What's up, bro? Y'all ready to head out. The car service pulled in behind me."

"Yeah, we're ready. Tell me you got some trees on you. Tasia is about to drive me crazy with all that fucking nagging."

"Since you talking, nigga, I won't be gagging either!"

"Really, Tasia? You really gone say that like I'm not standing here?"

"Oh, grow up, Keizon! Don't your wife suck dick?"

"Yeah, nigga! You think your sister doesn't knock a nigga down?" I laughed, looking at his shocked expression.

"Let me get the hell out of here. I'll see y'all at the safe house." We dapped it up, and Keizon walked out of the house.

I followed Tasia into the kitchen and observed her going

through the mail.

"Here, this is for you. It doesn't have a return address." She handed me the letter and observed it, but instead of opening it. I handed it to her.

"Throw that shit out. If we don't know who it came from, we don't give a fuck about what's inside."

"Are you sure?"

"Yeah, I'm sure. Let's go. The car service is out front."

Honestly, I felt like whatever was inside that envelope was going to piss me off. I was already up to my neck with bullshit, and I didn't want to deal with anything else.

ↄ ↄ ↄ ↄ ↄↄ

We were on the road about thirty minutes later and headed to the safe house. Latasia had been unusually quiet since we left. I know she hated the fact that we had to leave our new crib. She had to know that her living quarters on the Prince Compound were going to be top tier. I wanted to talk to her about having to leave for days at a time, but I'm already knowing she's going to swear I'm on bullshit with some bitches. I swear I'm not on that shit no more. When I said "I Do" I meant that shit. I've fucked with women from all walks of life, but none of them compared to my beautiful wife.

"This will all be over soon, and we will be back home. I'm doing this to make sure you and my son are safely tucked away. I promise to make it up to you when all this shit is over."

"I know, Horse. I'm so scared now. I've never worried about you not coming home. Getting that call about the explosion scared the fuck out of me. I instantly became sick, Horse! Baby, I was crying like you were dead. That was the worst feeling in the world. You don't have to make anything up to me. Just promise me you're going to come home to us."

"Stop crying. I promise to always come home to you." I firmly gripped her face so that she could see that I was dead-ass serious.

After placing a kiss on my lips, Tasia laid her head on my shoulder. It was crazy as fuck that a nigga was happy to see her show raw emotions. Her feistiness turned me on, but this soft girl era she was in had me wanting to tie her up and fuck the shit out of her.

Chapter 5: Tasia

I had been trying my best to be strong and not show fear. However, I was scared as fuck. The idea that someone really sent a bomb to kill them had me shook as fuck. All I keep thinking about is if Horse and Draylon had died. What in the fuck would Kateevah and I do? Our kids would be fatherless, and we would be single fucking mothers. The glitz, glamor, and luxury of being married to rich niggas was everything. However, we'd never really sat and grasped the fact that they were rich and powerful, not to mention hated. You had to truly hate someone to send a bomb to their place of business.

This shit had me shook, and Horse was too fucking calm for me, which meant the crazy nigga was plotting on some get-back. All I know is that he had better not die on me, or I would kill his ass. At first, I was so upset about us having to come to a damn safe house. Horse and I had finally moved into the home of my dreams, so a bitch was not trying to leave it. However, they had really put this place together.

Of course, the house we were in was right next to Kateevah and Draylon, which helped because I got to spend more time with my best friend. Right now, she definitely needs me to try to cheer her up. Her ass had been in a funk since that damn fight, not to mention this happening to Draylon. She had to put her feelings on the back burner and take care of him. Now that he and Horse were doing better, we could have our girl time. Honestly, I needed her expertise right about now. However, I knew that she needed me more, so I wasn't going to overwhelm her with my shit. Lord knows she always had to deal with me and my issues. I just wanted to be here for her right now.

I had been thinking about the letter since we'd left the house. It was addressed to Horse, but there was no return address, which I find weird as fuck. The fact that he threw it away piqued my interest, so when he wasn't looking, I retrieved it from the trash. With everything going on, I think he should see what the damn contents were. Hopefully, it was no damn anthrax or no shit like that. Hopefully, it was nothing that would make me lose my fucking mind. It had been more than enough bullshit dealing with the Prince family.

↘ ↘ ↘ ↘ ↘↘

"You couldn't wait until I made it before you started drinking." I laughed, observing Kateevah knock back a shot.

"You were taking too long. Here, take a shot so you can catch up."

"Blame Horse. That nigga waited well until I put my clothes on and wanted to fuck. You know I'm not turning down no dick." I knocked my shot back and sat on the bar stool next to her.

"You're not wrong. Where is my god baby?"

"Over at the house with Granny. Apparently, she'll be staying with us."

"I know. Annalise is going to stay over here with us. I'm glad because she is so good with Unique and DJ. Plus, she can help with Draylon's mean ass. I swear that fucking bombing made him even meaner. That nigga is the reason I'm really drinking."

"Speaking of Draylon. How are things with y'all?"

"Honestly, I haven't even been dwelling on the bullshit. The thought of losing him had me so scared that I literally waved the white flag. Life is too short. I know we will eventually have that much-needed conversation. I'm not worried about that lawyer bitch or her pressing charges. I'm in a I-don't-give-a-fuck mode. So, it's whenever and whatever. Draylon had better handle it. That's it. That's all. If the bitch calls herself being on some bullshit, I'm going to disfigure that bitch some more. The days of folks playing in my face are over with. No more nice Kateevah, and I mean that shit."

"I know that shit right. I'm so glad that you aren't all sad and shit. I've been kind of worried about you. Let's take a shot to not letting bitches play in our faces." I poured both of us a double shot, and we knocked them back. I loved to hear my friend standing on big fucking business.

"So, y'all getting drunk without me?" Belladonna quizzed, walking into the kitchen. I swear she loves her titties out. I'm sure my brother is having a damn hissy fit about it, too.

"Heyyyy, Ma! I didn't know you were coming out here. Why didn't you tell me?" Kateevah was all over Belladonna.

A little pang of jealousy hit me as I observed them embrace. It hurt that I didn't have that with La-La. For a minute, I thought we had made progress, but then she just up and left without notice. I could understand if she needed to get away and work on herself. What I didn't understand was her stopping communication. It made me feel like I had done something I wasn't aware of. Like, I knew I had been being a bitch to her during my pregnancy. I really hated I gave her a chance to be a mother. She disappointed and hurt me, but I'd never let her play with my love again. I'm done with La-La, so she could stop calling because I have nothing to say to her ass.

"How are y'all holding up?" Belladonna asked with a concerned look on her face.

"I'm good. Just ready to go back to my own house," I answered. "For the most part, I'm good, Ma."

"Listen, I've decided to stay here for a couple of days. Keizon has to make a run with Draylon and Horse, so I came out here to keep y'all company and help with the kids. Plus, I didn't want to be in the city by myself. With your ass fighting and going to jail, and then this fucking bombing, the shit has my nerves bad as fuck. All I keep thinking about is y'all and them babies."

"Tell me about it," I added.

"What's up, Kateevah? Come here, sis. Let me rap with you for a minute." Keizon gestured for me to follow him out onto the patio.

"Is everything good?" I inquired.

"Yeah, everything is fine. Listen, you need to answer the phone for La-La."

"Why do I have to answer the phone for her? She is the one who wasn't answering the phone for me, so I'm good on her ass."

"La-La is really going through it right now. I need you to at least pick up the phone and talk to her."

"I'm lost. Why are you so adamant about me talking to her? She stopped communicating with you, too," I reminded my brother.

Keizon had gone from being mad as fuck at her to being close as hell with her. I was confused because she had ignored his calls as well. One would think he would have an issue with her ass, too.

"I'm adamant because she's your fucking mother. Now answer the fucking phone for her when she calls again! You hear me, Tasia?"

"Clearly, you've forgotten I'm not your wife or child. Don't yell at me or tell me what to do. I'm tired of La-La not being a mother. Fuck her, and fuck you, too, for making me feel bad about choosing me. You and Horse keep saying fuck me and my feelings. I'm grown, but I need my mother too.

"Stop crying, sis!"

"Let me go!" Keizon tried to grab me, but I yanked away from him. I couldn't believe I was crying over La-La. For so long, I had kept my emotions hidden regarding this situation.

"Tasia, where the fuck are you going?"

"To the house. I need a minute, Dayvion!"

I didn't mean to snap at my husband, but now I was lowkey mad at his ass too. He and Keizon were dead wrong for trying to make me be nice to La-La. I loved my momma, but I couldn't keep letting her fuck with me for convenience.

"Tasia!" I stopped in my tracks, hearing Kateevah calling me.

"I'm good. I just need a minute."

"Your ass is not good. Let's go inside and talk about what got you mad. Look, I have the bottle."

I didn't respond until we got inside the house. Without hesitation, I grabbed the bottle from Kateevah.

"Keizon pissed me the fuck off, telling me to answer the phone for La-La. She's the one who stopped answering my calls. Now, all of a sudden, she's calling and wants me to answer. Fuck that! I'm tired of her never choosing to be a mother. I know I'm grown, but I still need my mother. You're my best friend in the whole wide world, so I know you won't judge me when I say this. When I just saw you and Belladonna embracing. It made me feel a little jealous. From the moment I met you, she has always been in your life. I've never seen her miss a milestone. As much as I couldn't stand your mom nagging us, I always had this love and admiration for her because she cared. La-La didn't give a fuck what I did. Belladonna did, though, and that meant something to me. Had your mom not been on me, I wouldn't have graduated from grammar or high school. Like I had a mother who was alive and well, yet she never showed up for shit. Now, I'm a mom and wife. She just doesn't get that I still need her. I've always needed her. I just don't understand."

The tears that I was currently shedding felt like buckets of water. I'm sure I was shedding all the tears that I had held in over the years. It's hard being strong all the time.

"Don't cry, Tasia. We both know La-La hasn't been good since your dad died. I'm positive she loves you. It's just that she doesn't really know how. As far as her just leaving and cutting off communication, there has to be an explanation. Something is off with the whole thing if you ask me. She was so happy about building a relationship with you and Keizon, not to mention being a grandma. I think you need to answer the phone for her. That's the only way you'll know. Now stop crying. It's freaking me the fuck out. I'm the damn crybaby in this friendship."

I couldn't help but laugh at Kateevah. She was right. Her ass was definitely the crybaby between us.

"I love you, friend. Thank you so much. I really needed that." We embraced one another and knocked back some more shots.

"I love you too. There is no need to thank me. You have always been the most supportive friend ever. Let's go back to the house so we can eat."

After cleaning my face, we headed back over to Kateevah's house. On the way, I decided I was going to go ahead and answer for La-La the next time she called. All I know is that she had better have a good ass explanation for this shit. If not, I'm going to put the idea of a mother/daughter relationship with her on the shelf. I'm a wife and a mother now. I have to focus on the family I'm building. One thing is for sure, and two for certain, Dayvion Jr. will never grow up feeling like he doesn't have a mother.

Chapter 6: Kateevah

Although I was still in my feelings with Draylon, I was so happy he was here with me and our kids. Lord knows if he had died in that bombing. I wouldn't know what to do. As I lay beside him, I can't help but thank God for covering him and Horse. He's managed to heal quickly, but the impact of the blast fucked up his back. I feel like he's overdoing it, but he insists on getting some get-back. My ass was regretting telling him to stay in the game. It's all fine and dandy when everything is great, and life is so fucking good. Now, they're basically at war with outside forces. Yeah, this shit is really scary.

Still, I know that I have to be a supportive wife. My husband needs me more than anything, and I'm going to stick beside him. However, I'm not over the way he handled me with that lawyer bitch situation. Both of them are still gone feel my wrath. He may think I'm green and don't know what's going on. I'm sure that bitch is trying something slick and underhanded as we speak. The bitch better be ready 'cause I definitely am. This shit lets me know I have to step my game up with the way I handle shit. I'm not a weak woman. I just love the fuck out of my nigga.

That bitch would love to have my husband and me to fall out. That bitch wants my man. As the bitch spoke to me, I really could see the green-eyed monster in her eyes. The bitch is jealous of me. She was looking at me, hating that I was everything she could never be or have. I had to sit and really dig deep within myself. Just because I'm a BBW doesn't mean I have to settle. The audacity of that bitch to think I had to pay that nigga to wife me.

Every time I think about it, I get angrier. The shit she said to me ignited a fire inside of me that no one wants to experience. That hoe done bought it up out of me, and it's up going forward. Draylon has assured me that he has the situation under control, so I trust that he knows how to handle the situation.

↘ ↘ ↘ ↘ ↘↘

The Next Day

"Let me talk to you for a minute," Draylon spoke as he walked into the kitchen dressed in all black. He was getting ready to be gone for a couple of days, which I didn't like at all.

He leaned me up against the counter and invaded my personal space.

"Look at me, Kateevah." He gripped my chin and forcefully made me look at him before kissing me on the lips.

"What's up?"

"I don't want you to be worried about me. We have some leads behind who did the bombing, so it's imperative we handle things before niggas get to skipping town. I might not be able to check in every hour on the hour, but just know that I will call and let you know that I'm okay. If I've never told you before, I want you to know that I love and appreciate you for nursing me back to health. Not only that, but I also appreciate you for being an amazing wife. I don't deserve you, but I love the fuck out of you. Do you know that?"

"Yes."

"I'm serious. I need to hear you tell me that."

"Yes, Draylon. I know you love the fuck out of me."

"Tell me this. Do you love me?"

"Of course. I love you. I love you more than anything in this world. However, I'm not going to stand here and act like I don't feel some type of way with you. I'm still very much so pissed off about the way you handled me after that fight. You never asked me what happened. You straight started chastising me like I was your child. Draylon, you disrespected the fuck out of me more than once. However, I put that shit on the back burner. When I got that call that you were hurt in an explosion, I prayed the entire way to the hospital that you were okay. In that moment, nothing else mattered. All I knew was that I couldn't live this life without you. There was no way I could tell our kids that you weren't coming home, so I asked God to keep you here with your family. He answered my prayers, so there was no way I was going to be dwelling on the bullshit. For better or for worse, right?" Now it was my turn to yank him by the fucking face.

"Right."

"Good. We agree. Now, I need you to go out there and handle

that threat. When you come back home, I need you to work on treating me like your wife and not something you own. I deserve respect, Draylon. If you can't give me respect, then you have to let me be free. It's not fair for me to give you the utmost respect, and it's not reciprocated. I've held you down and kept your secrets, so you don't get to threaten me to make situations work in your favor. I didn't like how you did that to me. I'm not trying to nag you or stress you out before you leave. It's just imperative you understand where I'm coming from."

"Baby, I'm so sorry. I promise you from the bottom of my heart I'll do better. You're the best thing that ever happened to me. I never want you to feel like you're not valued or respected. You've got my word. I'll never threaten you the way I did. Truthfully, I've felt fucked up about the way I handled you. Do you forgive me?"

"Of course I forgive you. All I ask is that you bring your ass home unharmed. I'll hold it down here." I wrapped my arms around his neck, and we kissed each other passionately. For a minute, we stood hugging each other tight.

"You ready, bro?" Horse's rude ass interrupted.

"Yeah, I am. Let me love on my wife for a minute, nigga!"

"Shouldn't you be doing the same with Tasia?"

"Now, sis, You know I've been loving on her all night and two times this morning. Don't call her for a couple of hours. She got nailed to the cross." Draylon and I fell out laughing.

"Nigga, you wild. I'll check in later." Draylon kissed me once more, and they left.

I rushed to the front window to watch them pull out of the driveway. Draylon was dressed in all black, looking as good as ever as he placed his bag in the trunk. I prayed they handled things and made it back safely.

Once they pulled away, I stayed in the window, taking in the scenery. The property was sprawling and so beautiful. Anyone would love to live out here, but it wasn't home. I would much rather be at our own house, not to mention at my salon and nail bar. Thank God I hired good staff to run them while I was on an extended vacation. Honestly, I hadn't been back to the salon since

Draylon came and embarrassed the fuck out of me. He had the entire shop scared. I'm happy as hell he didn't kill Smooth, but The look in his eyes let me know he wanted to.

Since DJ and Unique were with my mother over at the property she was staying in, I decided to climb up in bed and read a good-ass book. I was also going to roll me a fat-ass blunt and get higher than a giraffe's pussy. For the first time in a long time. The house was peaceful and quiet, just like I liked it to be. Nothing was worse than trying to read a book with noise all around you. As I headed up the stairs, I stopped in my tracks, seeing that DJ had left the TV on inside his room. When I stepped inside, I noticed his bookbag on the bed.

At first, I thought nothing of it. I cut off the TV and got ready to head out, but something was nagging at me to check it. DJ hadn't been carrying one around, but seeing the bookbag kind of made me want to make sure his ass didn't have a gun in there. Although he was a totally different kid than before, you could never be sure.

I opened it and noticed notebooks and folders. Of course, my ass sat down and looked through it, especially seeing that the notebooks didn't belong to him. Before looking through the pages, I made sure to observe the bookbag again. It was definitely the same bag from when he first arrived. I never went through it. Draylon did. He must have thought the folders and notebooks were DJ's things.

I quickly rushed to my bedroom and flamed up a blunt. For some reason, I felt like whatever I was about to read. Having some weed would be well-needed. The first notebook read *Draya's Thoughts* on the front cover. A bitch didn't hesitate reading.

Today, I had to sit through another boring ass meeting with my father. This shit was starting to get on my fucking nerves. Don't get me wrong, I love my dad, but he has all this animosity toward Draylon. The shit is sickening. He knew stepping down was the right thing for the family. However, he has never really wanted to hand it over. Learning that he handed things over so that Draylon would fail shocked me. Our father has always walked around boasting about how Draylon was going to take over and run things. What my father didn't expect was for Draylon to run shit better than him. My brother was securing deals with other factions that wouldn't give my father the time of day. He immediately became threatened, followed by going above and beyond to get the board to vote him out. He couldn't get it done without my vote or Granny.

I would have never gone against my brother. However, my father found out that I had been hiding DJ from Draylon. He threatened to tell him, so I had no choice but to betray my brother. He left me no choice.

It irritated the fuck out of me reading this. These motherfuckers were so selfish. Clearly, Draylon is great at what he does, yet his own father couldn't take it. Draya was too fucking weak to stand the fuck up. Keeping his son from him was downright wrong. She was judging her father, but that bitch was no better. There were more entries, but nothing really caught my eye until I came across an entry with my name in it.

I knew the moment Kateevah entered the picture that life was going to change for me. All the plans I had put into motion changed. I've never thought I would see the day my brother would go out sad behind a fat bitch like that. From the moment those bitches came around, I knew they were going to be trouble. I wanted to snatch them up and kill them, but Horse went off. Of course, he would have never gone against Draylon. Although Horse and I have a close ass relationship, he will never side with me over him.

That's the reason I never told Horse about the shit with DJ or the shit my father was up to. He wouldn't have hesitated to tell Draylon. Just when I had shit under control, things went left.

My plan was to be with Nautica when she came home. She, DJ, and I were going to be a family. I planned to simply walk away from my family and never look back. I'd always been in love with Nautica but was too afraid to let my family know. I was hurt when I found out she and my brother were fucking around. She has never really known that I have deeper feelings for her. My plan was to put it all out there when I picked her up from prison. I've never been interested in men. I've lied to her about the trysts I'm having with niggas. It was all a façade to keep her from learning that I was in love with her. I hated myself for fucking Shameeka. Both of us were on some drunk shit. My mother and Nautica talked on the phone from time to time, so I had to do damage control. Out of fear that my mother might tell her what she saw, I had to lie to her and say that it was actually my father who was fucking Shameeka. The last thing I needed was Nautica, knowing I had done that.

All I want is to be with her when she comes home, even though she's hellbent on being with Draylon, not to mention them being a family. I don't have the heart to tell her that won't happen. He has chosen Kateevah and that funny-looking ass little girl.

I knew that bitch didn't like me or my baby. It was a feeling I had deep inside that let me know. She never interacted with or acknowledged Unique unless Draylon wanted her to do something. I'm so happy Draylon killed that bitch. Reading this shit shows the hoe hated me and my daughter. It's a damn shame how people go out of their way to hate a person. The bitch didn't know me or my daughter. We're the best thing that ever happened to this family. Lord knows I shouldn't read anymore. Fuck it. The bitch has me intrigued.

I've fucked up, and there is no coming back from it. The worst thing I could have ever done was side with my father against my brother. Draylon was hurt. It hurt me to see the hurt in his eyes. There was nothing I could do about it, though. My father's plan to take over was already in motion. I had picked a side and knew it might cost me my life, which is why I'm ten steps ahead of my brothers. It's fucked up that I have to abandon DJ, but I taught him well. Draylon is requesting a sit-down. I'm sure my mother and Granny will be there as well, which is a good thing. He won't do anything crazy with them in the room. After this meetup, I'm taking DJ and disappearing until Nautica comes home. I'm done with this family and all the bullshit that comes with it.

I laughed reading this part because the bitch didn't expect Draylon to murk her dumb ass. I didn't even have to read anymore because it was nothing more to read. I decided not to even go back between the pages and read the other pages. Everything was self-explanatory.

Initially, I was going to keep the journals until Draylon came home so he could see this. Instead, I will put them back in the bookbag and place the bag right back the way I found it. Make no mistake. I'm going to tell him about it. The last thing I need is him finding out and thinking I'm keeping shit from him. Y'all know my husband is wired differently in the head. Speaking of my husband, I can't wait until he makes it back home. I miss him already. I'll be glad when all of this is over. I just want our lives to be normal again.

Chapter 7: Draylon

Getting word that the hit came from the Russians had me livid. At the same time, I was blaming myself for taking my time getting at them. With everything going on within the family, I had to put that beef on the back burner, which was a decision that could have cost us dearly. I simply couldn't let that shit just go like that. I've been trying my best to think of what the fuck the beef is. This shit is not about no fucking real estate deal that fell through. Not when I sent back the money that was given to my father, plus interest. Yeah, these motherfuckers got me fucked up.

"Bro, are you sure about moving on Nikolov? My source wasn't one hundred percent."

"It doesn't matter. I know his bitch ass is capable of it. Plus, he was some underhanded shit with your bitch ass daddy, so I'm not putting shit past him. If he wasn't the one behind it. I guarantee you he knows something."

"Hell yeah. He knows something," Keizon added.

When we pulled up to his restaurant, there were lots of cars parked and men standing out front.

"I should have known his bitch ass wasn't going to come alone."

"It's a good thing we got our people stationed all around this motherfucker," Horse stated, and we dapped it up.

The moment we stepped up to the door, a big-ass Russian nigga spoke while stopping us at the door. "You go in alone. Nikolav is alone ass well."

"Man, get your big ass out the fucking way! My brother is not going in there alone." Horse pushed the fuck out of him, which had all the other Russians pull out their guns.

I'm sure they thought it was just us three, but I had niggas on the roof ready to air them the fuck out. We easily could have given our people the sign to annihilate their asses, but that would have to wait until later.

"It's cool, bro." I gave both Horse and Keizon that look. They retreated, and I was led inside the restaurant.

The moment I stepped inside, I locked eyes with the servers,

Natasha and Kira, who had been working on the inside for me. Nikolav had sex trafficked them from Russia to over here. I offered them a way out, and they hopped on the offer. My back ached a little, and it angered the fuck out of me. Injuries to the back were no fucking joke. The doctor said it would be a while before I'm at one hundred percent, but the shit needs to hurry and heal. I'd been popping fucking pills like crazy, and I didn't like it.

When I finally made it to the back of the restaurant. I locked eyes with Nikolav. He looked sloppy as fuck with several plates of food in front of him. The nigga was damn near four hundred pounds and looked like he was about to burst. I'm sure a heart attack is in his near future if my bullets don't end his ass first.

"What can I do for you, Mr. Prince?" Nikolav spoke in his thick Russian accent and gestured for me to take a seat.

As much as I wanted to put a bullet in his fucking head, there was some shit that I needed to find out beforehand.

"You know why I'm here! Word is you're the one who sent that bomb to my place of business!" I gritted.

"Had I sent a bomb, you would be dead. Trust me when I tell you that didn't come from me. Truthfully speaking, it's your father who I wanted to kill. However, since you beat me to that, I'm content. Plus, I've already had a sit-down with your grandmother. She is still feisty and beautiful as she could be."

"What the fuck you mean you had a sit-down with my grandmother?"

"Listen, I'm not going to go into details about that. You'll have to speak with her. Just know and understand that I have no problem with the Prince family. As for the Ivanoff family, we have no beef with you all. Your granny extended the invite for me to remain on the council. You cleared your father's debt, so we're good. As a matter of fact, if my help is needed to find out who orchestrated that hit, say the word."

"Nah, we're good. As far as your seat on the council goes, my grandmother is no longer in a position where decisions like that can be made. That's my say. We can have another sit-down about that."

Before he could respond, I walked out, more livid than before. This is the shit I be talking about. Why would Granny go behind my back and make a call like that? Now I was right back at square one fucking around with her.

"What did that fat motherfucker say?" Horse asked when I stepped outside.

"We'll talk about it shortly. Let's ride back out to the safe house."

I honestly needed to think before I spoke about anything. Granny could have told me she talked to his ass before we came out here. I swear she had better have a good explanation, or the urge to strangle her old ass might finally take over. I'm so fucking fed up that I just might walk away from this shit.

↘ ↘ ↘ ↘ ↘↘

Hours Later

"Where the fuck is Granny at?" I didn't hesitate to go in the house looking for her slick old ass. Kateevah, Belladonna, and Tasia looked shocked as fuck at seeing us.

"What are y'all doing back so soon?" Tasia asked.

"Why? Let me find out you had a nigga pulling up or something."

"As sore as you got my pussy, nigga, I don't even want to look at another nigga. Since you're talking shit, I really was expecting to get some fucking rest!"

I wanted to laugh, but I was too busy trying to find my grandmother.

"Aye, bro, hold up!"

"Why y'all doing all of this yelling?" Granny asked as she came down the stairs.

"Come down to the man cave. We need to have a conversation!"

"Draylon, what's going on?" Kateevah questioned.

"Nothing, baby. We just need to talk."

"Are you leaving again?" Kateevah had a worried look in her eye, so I pulled her close and gave her a deep kiss on the lips.

"Nah, there's been a change of plans. Go fix a nigga something to eat." I smacked her on the ass and headed to my man cave. I'm happy as fuck she didn't ask any more questions.

"Slow down, Draylon!"

"Nah, you hurry up! Your old busy ass walked over and talked to Ivanoff, so you can walk fast and talk to me!"

The moment we walked inside the man cave, I slammed the door.

"Bro, not cool."

"Fuck that! I looked like a motherfucking fool sitting across from the Russian motherfucker!"

"Please tell me what the fuck happened when you went in there. What the fuck does Granny have to do with it?"

"Tell him, Granny! Tell Horse how you had a sit-down with Ivanoff!"

"Why in the fuck would you do that?"

"Both of you have a right to be upset, but don't disrespect me. I gave Ivanoff an offer he couldn't refuse: a standing seat on the council in exchange for leaving whatever beef he had with our family in the past."

"Bullshit! You were the main one saying that we should get at his ass! Now, all of a sudden, you go behind my back and cut a deal with the nigga. That's the shit I'm talking about. You're handing shit over to me, yet you're still heavily involved. I've put in too much work on the street for all this fake shit behind my back. As of right now, there is a new Prince family. None of them motherfuckers on that council are needed. I got my own fucking motion. I learned the hard way about being backdoored. As of right now and indefinitely, I'm no longer fucking with anything or anyone who has prior dealings with the old faction of the Prince family. I'm done. You with me, Horse?"

"No question!"

"You can't do that! I handed everything over to you!"

"Now I'm handing it back. You're my grandmother, and I love you. However, I will murk you if it comes down to it. That's the last thing I want to do, so let me walk away while shit is peaceful!"

I didn't give Granny a chance to say shit else. There was

nothing else to be said. I'll start this over before I keep killing family members and dealing with betrayal. Telling my grandmother, I would murk her doesn't feel good, especially since we've been on good terms. It's best for me to walk away and start my own shit, and that's exactly what I'm going to do. Honestly, I don't give a fuck who doesn't like it. I'm in the killing spirit, so any and everybody can get it.

↘ ↘ ↘ ↘ ↘↘

Later That Night

"Baby, are you sleeping?" Kateevah asked.

"Nah. I'm just lying here thinking. Did I wake you up thinking too loud?"

"No. I'm actually up thinking, too." I could hear the concern in Kateevah's voice, so I rolled over and wrapped my arms around her.

"What are you thinking about?"

"I feel bad for telling you to stay in the game. Life would be different for us had I never said that."

"No, you were being a supportive wife. Don't worry about shit. Life is going to be good for us. Let me worry about that. Just focus on your businesses, our kids, and being a wife. I got Prince's family affairs handled."

"I hear you. What about this situation with that lawyer bitch? You and I both know she's not going to just walk away easy. Have you talked to her?"

I went silent on Kateevah for a minute. Honestly, I was contemplating whether or not I should tell her about Javanna's offer. After everything she had been through, I know it's better if I go ahead and tell her. If she finds out later, I'm sure she'll lose her cool on a nigga. With us being in a better space, I want to keep it that way. Before telling her what the bitch Javanna wanted. I flamed up a blunt. I already knew Kateevah was gone lose her cool.

"Javanna said she'll drop the charges if I give her seed."

"That bitch said what? I see I'm going to have to whoop that bitch's ass again!" Kateevah jumped out of bed quickly. Her ass was acting like she wanted to swing on me. I flinched like a motherfucker.

"Calm down, baby! I would never do no shit like that. I'm going to see that the charges don't stick. Don't worry about it!"

"I'm not worried about it, but that bitch got me fucked up! I swear to God, I'm going to kill that bitch! She thinks I'm something to play with. Let me call Tasia 'cause we riding at dawn!"

It was hard as hell not to laugh at Kateevah. She was the preppy type, so she sounded funny cursing.

"You think this funny, and it's not! There is nothing funny about that Javanna bitch requesting that you get her pregnant. I'm not okay with this. That bitch wants you, and she can't have you. I'll gladly kill the bitch and do time. I'm really at whoever is trying to come between us. Like, I'm really tired of people thinking it's okay to play with me when it comes down to you. Just because I'm plus-sized motherfuckers think I don't deserve you as if they can love you better than me. Bitch, talking about I don't fit with you or your world. The whole time I am your world, and that hoe hates it! Ohhhhhh, I just want to beat that hoe up!"

"Chill out, Killa." I grabbed Kateevah around the waist.

"I'm serious, Draylon. That soft shit I've been on is over with. Motherfuckers got me fucked up!"

"I don't like you talking like that. It's not you. Baby, you aren't the type of woman who chooses violence. I love that about you. You're always talking about how you love your soft life and how you're in your soft girl era. Stay that way. Don't worry about what motherfuckers think. I don't care about the shit, Kateevah! "

"Of course, you don't care. To the world, you're the infamous Draylon Prince. Niggas want to be you, and bitches want to be with you. Baby, you have no idea about how hard it is for me. Everywhere we go, people stare at us. People are wondering why a man as fine as you want to be with a plus-sized woman like me. This is not about my insecurities. It's about people trying to make me feel insecure about my place in your life. That lawyer bitch basically said I paid you to be with me! That pissed me off. Honestly, that shit hurt my feelings a little, but I'll never give her the satisfaction of knowing that. I'm sorry I lost my cool in front of your business associates, but I couldn't let her treat me like that, Draylon."

"You don't have shit to be sorry for. I'm sorry for not hearing you out. That bitch is going to be even sorrier she came at you, anyway. Trust me! You don't have to worry about the people on the outside and what they think. I choose you, and I show the world that it's you. Look at me, them bitches can't fuck with you. That's why they come at you like that. Every time a bitch steps wrong, make that hoe step right."

"So, you're not gone be mad if I fight?"

"Nope. You just better win, or I'm gone fight you. My wife can't be out here losing fights."

"Oh please, Draylon. Belladonna taught me how to fight. Growing up, I just never liked to fight. Then I met Tasia's crazy ass, and she never gave me a chance to fight. Her ass was beating people up before I could react. No, seriously, though. I'll never be out here in these streets just fighting. I will only resort to fighting when I'm provoked, so don't even be worried. At the end of the day, I'm still a businesswoman, and I never want to hurt my brand or your business."

"Speaking of my business. I'm walking away from my family and starting my own Prince organization. How do you feel about that?"

"I support whatever it is you want to do. If you don't mind me asking, why are you doing that?" Kateevah climbed back on the bed and started massaging my shoulders.

"I can't trust Granny or my mother. Too much shit is going on behind my back, and I don't like it. I'm not sure who sent the bomb now. I was positive it came from the Russians, but after having a sit-down today, I learned it didn't come from him. To make matters worse, Granny promised him something she had no right to. I'm the head of the family, but they're always going behind my back. I'm going to end up killing them, so it's better that I walk away. I can no longer worry about that anymore. It's about the future of us and our kids."

"I got your back, baby, and I'm here for anything you need.

It's great that you're choosing yourself and being strong about transitioning. At the same time, I know it hurts not being able to trust them. Everything is going to be okay."

Kateevah started kissing me all over my neck as she hugged me tightly around my neck. Hearing her give me reassurance was all I needed to move forward with my plans.

Chapter 8: Belladonna

After spending a week kicking it with Kateevah, I finally came back home, which felt good as fuck. The house we stayed in on the Prince Family Estates was nice as fuck. However, I love our home in the city. It's like Keizon and I are in our own little world. Don't get me wrong. I loved living on that property near my daughter. However, that's her life, and I want her to be able to handle things without my help. If I let Kateevah, she'll come to me all the time needing help with how to deal with her husband.

I'm actually glad to know that she is taking charge of things and being stronger. The stronger she gets, the more respect she'll get from Draylon. Still, one thing is for sure and two for certain: he had better handle that lawyer bitch. I'm not really feeling her fucking with my daughter like that. Kateevah doesn't bother anyone. I'm happy as fuck she whooped that ass, but I'm even happier knowing she's standing up to Draylon's ole mean ass. I'm proud of the change I see in her.

Outside of that, Life for Keizon and me is the best it's ever been. Sometimes, I feel some type of way when he's out in the streets, but that's some shit my old ass has to get used to. For so many years, I had been alone, so I lived my life a certain way. With us being married, I've had to reconstruct my daily life. I would be lying if I said that the shit hasn't been hard. At the same time, Keizon makes it so easy to be with him. Outside of him being insanely jealous, he is really the best husband I could ever ask for. He's so much more mature than any older man I've dealt with. Keizon is top tier in my eyes.

"What did I tell you about staring at me when I'm sleeping?"

I immediately pulled the covers over my head and started laughing.

"How do you always catch me?" I pulled the covers from over my head and observed him getting out of bed.

"I'm a light-ass sleeper, and you know that. Aye, look, I have to make this run for Draylon real quick, but I'll be back home later tonight."

I caught an attitude instantly. We were supposed to spend the entire day together. With him being gone all the time and me doing hair, we barely get to spend time together.

"Why can't Horse or Moe handle it? We were supposed to spend time together. I've made dinner reservations and planned something special for you later," I pressed.

"This situation is something only I can handle. Baby, I promise to make it up to you. I'm not supposed to tell you this, but Draylon is planning a big trip for everyone to Turks next week. It's a surprise for Kateevah, so don't go telling her," Keizon disclosed.

Hearing that news cheered me up. I was definitely about to go off on his ass, but Turks sounded nice. Plus, I'd never been there, so I was happy as fuck.

"I promise not to say anything. Since you'll be gone all day, I feel like I should go shopping. Give me some money, Keizon."

"You went shopping a couple of days ago. What in the hell do you need?"

"I don't know yet. When I get to the mall, I'm sure they will have plenty of things I need. Money, please!" I held my hand out and waited for him to give me some money. Had he kept our date plans, he wouldn't have to give me money.

"Get whatever you want out of the safe and make sure you cop me some shit, too. I didn't see not one bag for me in the fucking closet."

"Oh please, Keizon! I always buy your stuff when I go shopping. Thanks. Please be careful and make sure you check-in." I grabbed him by the face and kissed him deeply.

"I will. Call me if you need me and pay attention to your surroundings. Take your gun with you." He gave me another peck and left out of the room.

I didn't waste time grabbing ten thousand from the safe. I'm about to shop until I drop. While grabbing the money from the safe, I heard my phone go off. Rushing over to my nightstand, I grabbed it and glanced at the screen.

Big Donna: *Hey, daughter. I'll be in town this weekend. I would love to see you and my granddaughters.*

I quickly put my phone down and didn't respond. My mother

was the last person I wanted to see. We've never really had a close relationship. She was the type of mother who fell in love with every man she encountered, which meant she moved from state to state quite often. My grandmother had to raise me because she chose being a wife over being a mother. I've never harbored any hard feelings. I just chose to live my life like she didn't exist. The exact way she did me.

The last time we talked. I learned my mom was on her fifth husband and living in Houston, Texas. All I could do was wonder why she was coming to Chicago. She doesn't know us like that. Plus, she doesn't know I'm married. Knowing her, she'll have something unsupportive to say, which will piss me off. It's better if I don't respond at all. Life was good and I didn't want her coming around shifting my positive mood.

⅄ ⅄ ⅄ ⅄ ⅄⅄

Days Later

The sound of La-La's voice made me sit up. I was knocked out and tired as fuck, so the last thing I wanted was to hear her fucking mouth. For the past week, I had been doing so many heads. I'd been a beautician for over twenty-five years, and I had never been so tired in my life. Everything on my body hurts, so I'm definitely not in the mood to deal with La-La. Whenever her ass is around, it's some bullshit. I'm going to be pissed if Keizon invited her without telling me. His ass has fallen back under her spell, and I'm angry about that.

"Belladonna! Girl, wake up! Your mother-in-law is here!"

I beat the fuck out of the bed, hearing her knocking outside of my door. It irritated me like hell when she insisted on saying she was my mother-in-law. It crawls my fucking blood.

"I didn't remember saying come in," I sassed.

La-La walked into my room and sat right on the edge of the bed. I sat up and tried to hold in my laughter. This lady was really crazy as fuck. Her head looked a hot ass mess.

"I need you to do my hair. Look at me, Belladonna. Them country bitches down there can't do no hair. I asked that bitch for a simple 27-piece with finger waves on the side, and she fucked me up. Why the fuck are you laughing? This shit ain't right. Please do my hair!"

"I have a head at twelve, so come about three o'clock, but don't think you're getting in my chair for no damn 27-piece and finger waves. I'm not doing that shit."

"I don't care what you do. Just fix this. I'm paying, too."

"Nah, it's on me. Now get out of my room. I need to get another hour of sleep."

"Bullshit! You better get your big booty ass downstairs and cook for my baby. He's eating peanut butter and jelly."

"I cook for my man every day. You're his mother, so I'm sure he would like you to do it for a change."

"I didn't come here to work. I'll see you at three. Thank you, daughter-in-law."

"Get out, La-La!"

I threw my remote toward her, and she rushed out of the room. I'm sure La-La was about to stress me the fuck out. At the same time, I was happy she was here so that she and Tasia could talk. It was time they both come clean about that Lynwood situation. Keeping that shit from her wasn't doing anything but making the situation worse.

↘ ↘ ↘ ↘ ↘↘

Beauty By Belladonna

It was well past three o'clock, and La-La still hadn't shown. If her ass didn't come by the time I was done cleaning, she was gone be assed out. All I wanted to do was go home and chill. Kateevah had me reading them crazy ass Urban Fiction books, and I was hooked. I'm about to sip some wine and read *His Love Is One In A Billion.*

As I swept up hair from the floor, the shop bell rang. I looked at the cameras and saw it was a female. Without hesitation, I buzzed her in.

"Hello, can I help you?" I asked her.

"I wanted to know if you did walk-ins." As she spoke, I observed her looking around the shop.

"I'm sorry, we're by appointment only. Would you like to make an appointment? I have open availability all this upcoming week." There was no way I was about to do her hair today. Honestly, looking at it, I realized she didn't need her hair done. She was rocking a really cute bob.

"Will Keizon be here any of those days?"

"Excuse me?" I had to make sure this bitch had really asked about my husband.

"Look, I'm not really trying to book with you, ma'am! However, I am here looking for Keizon."

"Wait a minute. Who the fuck are you, and why are you looking for my husband?"

"Your husband, huh? That nigga got me fucked up. Has he ever told you about me?"

"Bitch, are you crazy or something? I don't have the slightest fucking clue who you are. Clearly, you're here with an agenda, so tell me who the fuck you are and why are you looking for my husband?"

This bitch was definitely a couple of bricks short of a building. Her entire demeanor had changed. If Keizon had been cheating on me with this psycho, I swear I was going to kill his ass.

"I'm Myeisha! The bitch who held him down while he did that bid! I lost my job for that nigga. He made me promises and didn't make good on them. That nigga got me pregnant and disappeared on me. Come to find out, he done married some old fat bitch! Call his bitch ass before I nut the fuck up in here." She pulled a gun out of her purse and pointed it at me. I regretted leaving my gun in the car.

"Listen, I'm not sure about anything that you're talking about. You need to put that gun down, and we can talk about it." I didn't care about the crazy bitch calling me fat or old. I want her ass to get the fuck out of my shop.

"Nah, I don't want to talk! Every time you refer to my man as your husband, it angers me!"

"I don't know what happened between you and him when he was locked up. All I know is that he came home and proposed to me. Whether you like it or not, Keizon is my husband."

"Stop saying that!" she seethed and shot me in the chest. I didn't really feel the pain until I looked down and saw blood pouring out of a small hole.

"You shot me!"

"See what you made me do! He's not your husband. Say it before I shoot your old ass again!" My mind wanted to try to say the words, but the pain had crippled me. All I could do was fall to the floor, clutching my chest. I felt like I was going to pass out. Before I lost consciousness, I heard more gunshots.

Chapter 9: Keizon

It had been a week since Belladonna was shot. Miraculously, she was going to survive, but she was in a medically induced coma to help her heal. I don't know what I would do if I had lost her. All I kept thinking about was if she had got hurt behind some shit I was doing in the streets. However, I knew for a fact I'd done nothing to ruffle any nigga feelings to the point where he would want to hurt my wife. The police had been coming around every day to see if she was able to talk, but we just kept turning their asses around. Honestly, I wanted to be the first person to talk to her when they brought her out of the coma so that I could murder the motherfucker who hurt her. Jail time would be too easy. It was a must that I slowly tortured whoever did the shit.

"Hey, bro, I'm here for the night. Go home and get some rest."

"Nah, I'm going to stay the night. I told you that." I sat up in the recliner next to Belladonna's bed. Tasia was so hardheaded.

"I know, but you've been here all week. You and Kateevah need rest. Please let me sit with her. I promise if there is any change, I'll call. Please go get some rest."

"Sis, I'm not going to be able to rest until my wife wakes up! I need to know who the fuck would hurt her! Belladonna didn't bother anybody, and she didn't deserve that. They didn't take any money or anything of value. Someone went there with the intention to hurt her."

"I'm sure you'll get to the bottom of it. In the meantime, you need to get some rest and clean yourself up. We both know if she wakes up seeing you looking like a caveman, she'll have a fit." That made me laugh a little because it was the truth.

"Thanks, sis. I needed that laugh. Call me if anything changes."

"I will. Oh yeah, tell your momma to kiss my ass," Tasia stated.

I just shook my head and walked out of the room. I'm not going to go there with Tasia now because she's being a brat. I'll be glad when La-La comes clean about why she got away for a while. I already know shit is going to hit the fan when Tasia finds out about Lynwood. At this point, I want her to know everything so that we can move forward. Life is really too short. Right now, I can't even deal with that. My only focus is Belladonna.

↘ ↘ ↘ ↘ ↘↘

After getting a good night's rest, I made a couple of business runs around the city. It was imperative I handled shit and got to the hospital. Belladonna's doctor was going to start the process of bringing her out of a coma, and I wanted to be the first person she saw when she opened her eyes. Once my baby gets well, I plan to take her on a month's long vacation.

"What's up, Keizon? Long time no see."

As I headed into the liquor store I owned, I bumped into Myeisha. No lie. My heart started to race. Seeing this bitch irritated the fuck out of me. She was crazy as hell. I regretted fucking on her when I was behind the wall.

"Hey, Myeisha." I tried to walk past her, but she grabbed my arm.

"Really, Keizon? That's all you have to say to me."

"Bitch unhand me! What the fuck do you want me to say?"

"Why haven't you reached out to me? I've waited all of this time. You promised me when you came home, we would be together!" *Yeah, this bitch had lost her mind.*

"Myeisha, let me make myself very clear. You never had a chance in this lifetime of being with me. Honestly, you aren't my type. I was a nigga in jail who needed someone on the outside to help me move my shit. If memory serves me right, it was you, Officer Brooks, who approached me. It's not my fault you fell in love with dick that could never be yours. You're a pick-me-ass bitch, which makes you're weak in my eyes. You're the type of woman a nigga walks all over strictly off the fact that you're willing to do anything for a nigga to pay you attention. Your ass was a correctional officer who did favors for numerous fucking inmates. The moment you came to me about being pregnant with my seed, I knew you were delusional. I immediately cut you off, and you lost your fucking mind."

"No! No! No! I lost my job because of you!" Myeisha angrily shouted.

"Crazy bitch, you lost your job because you crossed a line no correctional officer should ever cross. I never told you we would be together, so don't say that shit again."

"Okay, fine. You don't have to want to be with me, but please be there for our daughter. Her name is Keirra, and she just turned three. I'm telling you, she's your daughter. I wasn't fucking with anyone else."

"Get that fucking phone out of my face, bitch, and go find out who your real baby's father is! Crazy ass bitch, I'm not him! Stay the fuck from around my business! Fuck on somewhere!" I pushed her ass out of my way and proceeded inside my store.

Myeisha had me so fucked up trying to play games with me. I swear I had a feeling the bitch was going to be a fucking problem.

↘ ↘ ↘ ↘ ↘↘

Northwestern Hospital

When I stepped into Belladonna's room, I was surprised to see an unknown woman in there with Tasia.

"Hey, bro, this is Belladonna's mom."

Hearing that kind of had me taken aback. I had never met Belladonna's mother. As a matter of fact, I've never really heard anything about the woman.

"Oh yeah. Nice to meet you. I'm Keizon, her husband."

"Hi. Excuse me for a minute," she spoke dry as fuck and exited the room.

"That lady is rude as fuck. Kateevah needs to hurry up and get back up here. She was actually trying to get me to leave the room," Tasia ranted.

"Why the fuck you didn't call me?"

"Because I knew you were on your way already. Plus, I wasn't letting that bitch make me leave."

I didn't hesitate to walk out of the room to see where she went. When I made it to the nurses' station, I observed her speaking with the nurses, and there were also security guards.

"Is there a problem?"

"Yes. There is a problem. I don't want any outside people visiting my daughter. I've heard nothing about her being married."

"I don't give a fuck what you didn't hear about! That's my wife, and I'm the only person who has the power to say who can visit. As a matter of fact, bitch, I don't know you, so now you can't fucking visit!"

"Keizon, what's going on?" Kateevah asked as she stepped off the elevators.

"Ask your grandmother. While you're at it, tell her exactly who I am because she got me fucked up!"

I didn't intend to get loud with Kateevah, but I'd be sure to apologize later. Still, she really needed to let her grandmother know what the fuck it was and what the fuck it wasn't. I couldn't care less if that was Belladonna's OG. She won't disrespect me. The moment I stepped back into the room, my mood shifted.

"Look, she woke up."

Belladonna's eyes were open. I didn't hesitate to rush over to her bed. My heart damn near stopped seeing the tears pouring out of her eyes. "Why are you crying?"

Belladonna started to get excited, which made the machines start to beep like crazy. Shortly after, the hospital staff rushed in and started examining her. Tasia grabbed my hand and pulled me out of the room.

"Is my momma okay?" Kateevah began to panic.

"No. She's fine. Her eyes are open. They're in the room checking on her now."

"Thank you, Jesus! Please forgive me for my rudeness. My granddaughter explained everything to me. I just didn't know. I apologize to you and your sister."

"It's cool. Look, I'm going to go get some air. I'll be back up in a minute."

A nigga needed to hit a blunt a couple of times. Seeing my wife awake and upset fucked me up. I'm not sure what it was about the look in her eyes, but it felt like she was reliving what had happened for some reason. Either that, or she was just simply sad. It was like the tears started pouring out in full force the moment she locked eyes with me. That shit did something to me. Now I was more ready than ever for her to tell me who the fuck did this to her.

↘ ↘ ↘ ↘ ↘↘

Hours Later

It had been hours since Belladonna woke up, and she had yet to say anything to me, so I fell back and observed her talking with her mother and Kateevah. Of course, she was very weak in lots of pain, so I kept my thoughts to myself. Honestly, I was happy as fuck my wife was out of the woods.

"Visiting hours are now over! Visiting hours are now over!"

Are you going to stay the night, Keizon? If you can't, I'll stay the night," Kateevah offered.

"Nah, you go home and get some rest. I'm going to stay the night."

"It's cool. You can all go home. I'm sure you've been here around the clock. Plus, I'm so tired. That pain medication has me sleepy."

"I'm staying, Belladonna." I took a seat and started scrolling through my phone.

"Yeah, Ma. Somebody has to stay with you. Grandma Donna and I will come back tomorrow. Call me if you need to, Keizon." Kateevah kissed Belladonna, gathered her things, and left.

I observed her grandmother getting ready to say something. Instead, she followed Kateevah out of the room, which I was happy about. I was in no mood to curse her out again.

Once we were alone, I wasted no time moving closer to Belladonna's bed.

"Baby, you have to tell me who did this to you. I feel like you're avoiding me on purpose. Please, Belladonna, talk to me."

"She shot me because you're my husband. I don't want you here, Keizon. You cheated on me with some crazy ass obsessed bitch. I can't even remember her name. The only thing I remember is her shooting me."

"Listen to me, baby. I have never cheated on you. Belladonna, you know me. I love the fuck out of you. Just think. Do you remember her telling you a name or anything she said?"

"I think she said her name was Keisha or something like that. All I know is the idea of you being married to me enraged her. You promise you've never cheated on me. She said that you all have a baby together."

As I leaned in and comforted my wife, I knew exactly who had hurt her. It was that crazy ass bitch Myeisha. It was no coincidence that I bumped into her ass. Heated wasn't the word for the way that I was feeling. That bitch, Myeisha, played in my face. I'm mad at myself for not paying more attention. The moment she popped up out of the blue. I should have known she was behind that shit. I was slipping, and I didn't like that shit at all.

"Listen to me. The police are going to come tomorrow and talk to you. They've been here every day, hoping you're awake so that you can give a statement, but don't tell them shit. Act like you don't remember. I'm going to handle that bitch. I promise you, Belladonna, I've never cheated on you. I fucked with her when I was locked up. She helped bring shit in for me. As far as her having a seed with me, I don't believe anything that crazy bitch says. Baby, I promise you I'm going to make that hoe suffer for what she did to you. I love you. Please forgive me for being the reason someone brought harm toward you."

"I love you too, Keizon. However, I still want you to leave. It's not anything personal against you. I'm in pain, and I really do want to just sleep. I promise I won't tell the police anything."

It hurt me a little that Belladonna didn't want me to stay the night with her. At the moment, she was telling me one thing, but her body language was telling me something different. She was mad at me, and I could feel it in my heart. Still, as much as I wanted to go off, I knew I couldn't. She had just been through something traumatic, so all I could do was respect her wishes. Belladonna had to know that I wasn't going to allow her to just ice me out, especially when I hadn't done anything wrong.

"You got that. I'll be back to check on you first thing in the morning." I kissed my wife on the lips and left, headed out.

As I headed to the crib, I knew I had to get my hands on this Myeisha bitch. I was kicking my own ass for not knowing any personal information on her. If she knew like I did, her ass had better be on the first plane out of Chicago.

Chapter 10: Kateevah

If it wasn't one thing, it was another. Just when I started to think things were getting back to normal, something crazy happened. Getting the call that my mother was shot had me scared as fuck. The only thing I could think about was, what the hell would I have done if she had died? I've never imagined life without her, but one thing is for sure, and two for certain: God has to take me first because I can't live without her. Knowing that she will indeed make a full recovery has relaxed me, and I'm happy as hell that she's coming home. Unique is going to be so excited to see her grandma. My baby has been so sad this whole week.

"Kateevah, I need to talk to you," Granny stated the moment I stepped into the kitchen. Outside of dealing with my mother being shot, I had been dealing with the drama the Prince family had going on. I swear it was always some shit.

"Can it wait until later? I'm about to head over to the hospital. My mother comes home today, and I want to help Keizon get her settled in." The last thing on my mind was the drama going on with her and Draylon. Right now, all I want is to focus on my mother.

"I'll make it quick. Have a seat." Deep inside, I knew Granny was about to speak on this shit that was going on between her and Draylon.

"What's up, Granny?"

"Listen, I need you to talk to Draylon. He can't walk away from the family and start his own faction. That's not how this life works. For the sake of the family, I need you to get him to change his mind."

"I'm not doing that."

"What do you mean?"

"I mean just what I said. I'm not going to tell Draylon not to walk away. To be honest, I think he should walk away. After everything that he has been through, that man deserves to make some choices for the sake of himself. If he doesn't, he's going to lose his life behind your family. I'm not trying to be disrespectful. However, as his wife, it's my responsibility to look out for him since you and Annalise don't."

"You're crossing a line, Kateevah."

"That's fine. Behind my husband, I'll cross any line I want. You went behind his back and had him looking like a fool at that sit-down. Why would you go and do that without speaking to him first? If memory serves me right, you promised that he had full control over all things dealing with the Prince family. I'm sorry if you're feeling disrespected. However, you had no right to do that. After everything that Draylon has been through with his father and sister, the last thing he needs is more treacherous relatives. I'm sorry, Granny, but I will not try to change his mind. He's getting a new start, and you can thank yourself for that."

I stood up from the table and left her sitting there. Granny wasted her time trying to get me to change Draylon's mind. I'm supporting my husband's decisions one hundred percent.

⬎ ⬎ ⬎ ⬎ ⬎⬎

"Thank you so much, Tasia. I don't know where I would be without you."

"Oh, please. You know I love Belladonna's ole bougie ass." She laughed and continued to cook dinner.

"I heard that." I smiled, observing my momma walk into the kitchen.

"Ma. What are you doing up? Go lay back down."

"Please stop fussing over me. I'm fine. Plus, I've been lying down for over a week. I need to get up and stretch. Y'all asses better not scratch up my countertops."

"Baby, I'm about to run some errands. You need anything." Keizon asked and kissed her on the cheek.

"Nah, I'm good."

I observed my mother quickly walk out of the kitchen, and the look on his face was a hurt one. Ever since she has been awake and alert, she has been acting weird with Keizon. Initially, I wasn't going to say anything. However, I think I need to try to see what's going on with them. Plus, she keeps saying that she doesn't remember who shot her., but for some reason, I think that she's lying.

"Hey Tasia. Can we talk for a minute?"

"No, we can't. I'll be back, Kateevah." Tasia turned off the pots and walked out of the kitchen.

La-La just stood in place, looking as hurt as ever. For the first time, I felt sorry for her.

"Just give her some time. She'll come around and hear you out. You know how stubborn Tasia can be."

"Thanks, Kateevah. I know it might not seem like it, but I do love my kids. I'm never going to stop trying to make things right with Latasia. Right now, isn't the time for that, anyway. The most important thing is that Belladonna is okay. It's about her. Just know that I'm here to help in any way. I know she and I have had our differences, but that's all behind us now. Your mom is very important to my son, and I just want to be supportive. I promise I'm not here to hurt anyone. I'm just desperate to make things right."

Seeing La-La shedding tears made me rush over to comfort her.

"Don't cry. Everything is going to work out. Thank you for simply trying to make things right. It might not seem like it now, but that means a lot. I'm going to go check on my momma. Can you finish the food?"

"Yeah. I got you."

As I headed to my mother's bedroom, I observed Unique sitting on the couch, looking sad.

"What's wrong?" I took a seat next to her, and she climbed up onto my lap before laying her head on my shoulder.

"Grandma is sad, Mommy," Unique cried.

"Why is grandma sad?"

"She's sad because someone shot her. Why did they hurt my grandma?" Unique was having a full-blown meltdown, which made me cry as well.

"Listen, grandma is going to be just fine. Stop crying. I'm going to go cheer her up, okay? Go to your room and play on your iPad." I kissed her on the forehead, then proceeded up the stairs to talk to Belladonna.

When I stepped into the room, she was sitting on the edge of her bed.

"Don't come up here fussing. I'm okay."

"Ma, I didn't come up here to fuss. I actually wanted to talk to you. Unique is pretty upset about you being sad. I am, too. Please tell me who shot you. I know you know who it was."

"Please, Kateevah, just leave it alone. I don't want to talk about it, but Keizon is going to handle it."

"No. I'm not going to leave it alone. Tell me everything right now! I'm your daughter, and I should know!" I was looking upside her head like she was crazy.

"You can't say anything, though. I promised Keizon I wouldn't tell the police, so don't say shit."

"Okay, I won't."

"Some crazy ass female that Keizon was messing with when he was in jail is the person who shot me. She just was wilding and acting crazy as fuck every time I mentioned him being my husband. The bitch said she has a baby by him, Kateevah. I'm too old to be being attacked by some young bitch about him. The crazy part about it is that the look on her face before she shot me is all I keep seeing."

"Wait a minute. Has Keizon cheated with her since he's been home?"

"I don't think so. Whatever Keizon had going on with her happened while he was locked up, and it has that bitch crazy as fuck. What if she's telling the truth?"

"Don't worry about that crazy ass bitch. We both know Keizon is crazy about you, and he wouldn't cheat. Let's just focus on you getting well. Come on, lay down. All of this stressing is not going to help you heal. Let's let Keizon handle things. I'm sure she's just some infatuated female."

"Infatuated isn't the word. Delusional and bat-shit crazy better fit her ass. I'm telling you. That bitch was a woman acting off raw emotions. I'm not sure what she and Keizon had going on. Whatever the fuck it is has her willing to kill. I just hope he finds that bitch. For all I know, she has my home address," my mom ranted.

I remained quiet and helped her get into bed. There was so much I wanted to say, but I couldn't. This shit was crazy as hell to me. My mother should not be going through this. I'm pissed off. Still, I know Keizon would never cheat on her, not to mention he doesn't play about her. I'm sure he's getting down to the bottom of things as we speak. His ass just had better hurry and handle whoever the crazy bitch is. My momma has never shown any fear in her life, but looking at her, I could tell that bitch had scared her. I'm going to try my best not to say anything about this, but Keizon better kill that bitch for hurting my momma. I crawled up in bed beside her and laid with her until she fell asleep.

The sound of my grandmother Donna talking made me rush downstairs. From the moment she arrived, I could tell my momma was uncomfortable. Due to the circumstances, she allowed her to stay. That stunt my grandma pulled with Keizon has him not fucking with her. Even though she apologized, I don't blame him. She had no right to come at him and Tasia sideways. She doesn't know shit about my mother, so she definitely crossed the line.

Growing up, I never knew my mom to have a solid relationship with her. They would talk every now and then, so her presence had me questioning why she was here.

"How is Belladonna feeling?"

"She's sleeping right now. Did you find everything you needed in the guesthouse?"

"Yes, I did. Where is Keizon? I need to talk to him."

"He left, but I'm sure he'll be back later. You can talk to him then. I need to go pick up my momma's medicine. I'll be back. Do you mind keeping an eye on Unique for me?"

"Of course. My great grandbaby is fun to hang out with. She's been teaching me how to play Goldfish for money."

I couldn't do shit but laugh. My daughter was really a card shark. It's crazy how all the adults really sit and gamble with her. Never in my life have I witnessed a kid running card games, not to mention tricking them out of their money.

Chapter 11: Tasia

"Let me talk to you real quick. Come over here and sit down." Horse grabbed my hand and led me over to the bed. Instead of sitting down, he pulled me in between his legs and wrapped his arms around my waist.

"What's up?"

"I need you to talk to La-La. Baby, you can't keep walking around here being mean to her. That's not going to make you feel better."

"Why is everybody constantly telling me to make shit right with her? Please don't make me do it!" I started just shedding tears.

I'm sure I sound like such a brat right now. This whole situation makes me feel like a teenager yearning for a mother's love. I'm so mad at myself for caring. I wish I could go back to the old Tasia that didn't give a fuck about La-La's ass.

"Don't cry, baby. I'm not telling you this to make you upset. I'm telling you to have the sit-down so that you can speak what's on your heart. I'm not making you do shit that you don't want to do. I just think if you get it off your chest, you can move on. Clearly, she's going to be back around for a while. Eventually, you'll have to get the conversation out of the way. Stop crying and get dressed." I quickly wiped my face upon hearing that.

"Where are we going?"

"You'll know when we get there."

"What should I wear?"

"Get pretty."

"Nigga, I'm already pretty."

"Not with that wet ass face and that snotty ass nose!"

"Fuck you." I laughed and started throwing pillows at his ass. He dodged them all and rushed out of the room.

I was lowkey happy he told me to get dressed. A bitch was more than ready to get out of the house. Draylon has basically switched up the entire operation, which has Horse working around the clock. I'm not complaining because we're all back at our regular homes.

Outside of that, I've been worried about Keizon. That nigga

has been on a rampage looking for Myeisha's crazy ass. The first time I met up with her, she gave me bad vibes. I knew she was in love with Keizon, but she was literally the last person I thought was behind Belladonna's shooting. Honestly, the crazy bitch hasn't been a thought at all. I've always known Keizon never really fucked with her like that, so I'm positive he had never cheated on Belladonna. I'm praying he gets to the bottom of this sooner rather than later. That crazy bitch can't be out on the loose for too long.

ＮＮＮ ＮＮＮ

"Forever More" by R. Kelly blasted as Horse cruised Lake Shore Drive. It was a beautiful Spring night. If someone had told me I would fall head over heels in love with him, I would have said they were a lie. Don't get me wrong, the nigga still got demon dick, and I'll forever refer to him in that way. However, since we got married, he has changed so much.

Horse still loves to dominate me. I don't think he will ever not want to do that. Still, I can't explain it. All I know is that Horse shows me he loves being a husband and father. At first, I thought this man would come into my life and hurt me, yet Horse did the opposite. That man has completely changed my life. He actually gave me a little family of my own, which was something I never thought of. If there is anything I've learned from this, It's never to judge a man by his cover. Sometimes, the man of your dreams is underneath all of that. You just have to be the woman who chips away at the ice around his heart.

"You know I've been working on a special project, right?"

"Yeah," I answered as I turned the radio down and gave Horse my undivided attention. We exited the expressway and headed into Hyde Park.

"I decided to open our first family-owned business," he disclosed as he flamed up a blunt, and I looked at him like he was crazy.

"Horse, your family has numerous businesses."

"I'm not talking about the family I come from. I'm talking about the family that I created. Day in and day out, I've watched you be a mother and wife. However, I never see you do anything for yourself that's fulfilling. Don't get me wrong, I'm not saying that being a wife and mother isn't fulfilling. However, I want you to be more than just those things. We once had a conversation, and you told me that you would love to have an upscale supper club. Do you remember telling me that?"

"Yeah. I remember, but it was just an idea."

"Well, it was an idea that has become reality. Look up."

The moment I looked up through the windshield. A sign on a building lit up, and it read *Junior's Supper Club.* The red and gold trimmed lights basically lit up the somewhat dark block.

"I can't believe it. Are you serious about this, Horse? I don't know anything about running a club. What if it fails because of me?"

"Stop it, Latasia. If anything, you're going to be the reason it becomes a nationwide franchise. One thing about you is that you know how to play the game. You've been hustling your whole life alongside Keizon, so you know what it takes to bring money in. This is an upscale establishment, so only the elite of niggas can grace those doors. If you're not connected, then you cannot get in. It's not just for niggas. It's for boss-ass females, too. Latasia, you're a boss, so there isn't a doubt in my mind that you won't be great at running this motherfucker. This right here is our future and our son's future. When we leave this world, our kids will keep this shit going."

"You're going to make me cry, Horse. Who are you, and what have you done with my Demon Dick ass nigga?" We both laughed.

"I'm still him and don't you ever forget that. I just really want some shit that's solely ours. Plus, I'm not sure where the Prince family is headed. Of course, I know my big brother knows what the fuck he is doing. I'm one hundred percent sure he's about to take us to new levels. At the same time, I have to do the same for myself. I'll always be Draylon's right hand and the motherfucking muscle. However, I have to be my own boss with my own shit."

"I'm so proud of you. I know sometimes I give you a hard time. Hell, I know it can be hard loving my bipolar ass, but you, here it is, you're doing something that can generate me wealth. No one has ever made me feel like they believe in me. I appreciate you so much, and I'm grateful for you. Horse, I love you so much, and I want you to know that I thank God every day for bringing you into my life."

I didn't hesitate to reach over and wrap my arms around his neck before we passionately kissed.

"The inside will be finished in a couple of weeks. Then we can go in and have a good look at it. Don't worry, Tasia. Everything is going to be just fine. All we have to do is work as a team."

With all the reassurance Horse was giving me, it made me more comfortable with this whole business idea. I was lowkey nervous as fuck because I didn't know the first thing about running businesses. Yeah, I've hustled with the hardest of niggas, but it doesn't mean I'm a businesswoman. I've never thought about taking business classes. However, I think this is the perfect time to enroll in some courses. I wanted to show Horse I could succeed and make our business flourish.

ꓹ ꓹ ꓹ ꓹ ꓹꓹ

A Couple of Days Later

"Can I talk to you for a minute, Latasia?" I looked up to see La-La standing in the doorway of my bedroom.

"There is really nothing to talk about. Shouldn't you be headed to the airport? I thought you were heading back to Texas."

"Yeah, I am headed to the airport, but first, I wanted to say my peace. At this point, I don't give a fuck if you're choosing not to talk, but you will listen Latasia. The only reason I haven't tried to fight you behind the disrespect is because I owe you an explanation."

"You don't owe me shit. Bye, La-La!" I was serious as fuck at the moment. There was no need for her to explain. I'm sure it won't change anything, especially since she's getting ready to leave, anyway. What is the fucking point?

"I left because I couldn't handle the fact that I killed Lynwood."

Hearing her say that made me toss my computer to the side.

"Really, La-La? I mean, you have stooped to an all-new low. Daddy was killed in a drug deal gone bad."

"No. He wasn't. We were led to believe that for years, but your dad showed up out of the blue alive and well. The only thing about it was that he was here with an agenda against the Prince family. He was working with the fucking police to bring Draylon and Horse down. Keizon came to the house one day and found him there. I'm not going to lie. At first, I was just happy to have your dad back home, but then he started trying to convince Keizon that he needed to stop having dealings with Prince family. I knew something was off about it, so I just played along until I had enough evidence."

"How come you or Keizon didn't tell me that he was alive?"

"Because we know how much it would have hurt you. He wasn't genuinely back to be with his wife and children. Lynwood came back to destroy your newfound happiness. It was bad enough that I had checked out due to me thinking he was dead. There was no way he could make us suffer when we had all become a solid family again. I'm sorry we kept it from you. At the time, we thought we were making the right decision. Plus, we didn't want to mess up your life with Horse. Please don't be mad at Keizon. That's the reason I left. Latasia, I couldn't bear to face you knowing what happened. Not only that, but it also hurt me to actually kill him. However, I'm not apologetic for doing it. I'm only sorry about leaving and not telling you the truth. Now you hate me, and I don't think you'll ever forgive me."

When I looked at La-La, she was crying, which was something she rarely did. Reluctantly, I got up and hugged her. It was the right thing for me to do.

"We have to tell Horse and Draylon about that. If we don't, they'll think we were against them. They're big on loyalty, La-La." The idea of Horse thinking I would betray him in any way had me starting to panic.

"Horse knows already. He just hasn't said anything to you about it. Don't worry. When I came back into town, my goal was to come clean about everything, which was why he was trying to get you to have a sit-down with me. If there is anything that you want to get off your chest, please do it. No matter how hurtful it is. I just want you to get it off of your chest."

For months, I've gone over all the anger I've felt toward her. Right now, I can't even bring myself to curse her out. I felt sorry for her and pissed off at the same time. She and Keizon are wrong for keeping me out of the loop. For years, I've been the one who held them down when they needed me. Growing up young made me stronger. However, I was still a little girl who needed some shielding in their eyes. I could have very well-handled Lynwood's ass, especially knowing that he came back to hurt my man and his family. She wouldn't have to kill his ass because I wouldn't have hesitated to kill him. It's real fucked up he allowed us to suffer without him for all of those years.

"I'm sorry for being mad at you and giving you a hard time. It's just that you hurt my feelings when you left like that. For the first time in a long time, I had my momma back in my life, and it felt good. La-La, seeing you be a grandmother to Junior meant everything to me. When you up and left, I didn't understand it, so I decided I was done with trying to have a mother/daughter relationship with you. That's why I didn't want to talk to you. Now that you've told me why you left, I feel bad for refusing to talk to you."

"Don't feel bad. You didn't know. We never should have kept it from you."

"Just so you know, I am very pissed off about that. No matter what, I should have known that my father was alive from the jump. Trust and believe I'm going to cuss Keizon's ass out. Although I'm upset about it, I understand that you were doing it to protect me. Thank you." I wrapped my arms around La-La and hugged her tight.

"Let me get out of here before I miss my plane."

"Why don't you stay a little longer? I'll reimburse you for your flight. I'm sure Junior and Keizon would love that."

"Are you sure? Because I'm not dealing with your stank-ass attitude anymore."

"Yes, I'm sure. In my defense, I was mad at you. No, really. I want you to stay, Ma."

From the bottom of my heart, I meant it. Allowing my mom to leave without starting over would be wrong of me. Plus, I needed her to help with the supper club. It would be right up her alley to mingle with rich folks. I'm not going to lie. Horse was right. Having this conversation did make me feel better. It felt like a weight was lifted off my shoulders.

Chapter 12: Keizon

Since Belladonna had been home, her energy was so off. To keep from feeling some type of way, I stayed out all day and came home at night. I'm not about to be acting like a tender dick ass nigga all in my feelings. However, I wasn't feeling the way Belladonna was handling me. It didn't feel good knowing she was lowkey mad at me yet acting like she wasn't. It also dawned on me that Kateevah knew who shot her, so she had kind of been acting funny, too. I'm not mad about it, though. If it were my mother, I would probably feel some type of way, too.

Speaking of my mother. I'm glad she and Tasia are back talking. That's one less family problem that I have to deal with. Of course, Tasia was mad at me for not telling her about Lynwood. Honestly, I was not about to entertain her bratty ass. We did what we had to. I'm glad she knows, so now we can move forward and just live a good life with La-La's crazy ass. She has proven that she has changed and wants to be a mother, which is good enough for me.

"You good, bro?" Horse asked. We were at his crib in the man cave, chilling.

"Yeah. I just can't wait to get my hands on this Myeisha bitch. Shaw is supposed to get with me later tonight to share the info he's got." I poured myself a shot of Don Julio and flamed up a fat-ass blunt.

"I knew the bitch was going to be trouble when you brought her into that fold. Do you think she got a kid by you for real?"

"Hell nah, I don't believe shit that crazy ass bitch says. She's got my fucking wife thinking I was going to be with her deranged ass."

"You niggas starting without me?" Draylon stated as he walked into the man cave.

"We just opened the bottle, nigga. What the fuck took you so long?" Horse inquired.

"I had to have a meeting with the accountant. Some things needed to be moved around. Hand me the bottle. I need a fucking shot after going through the finances."

"Shit straight?"

"Yeah, nothing major. I had to put a cap on Granny and Annalise's spending. They got their own bread to buy that outlandish ass shit they like, but they've been spending money from accounts that they shouldn't even have access to. I know they'll be mad when they find out they've been cut off."

Every time I think about my family's problems, I try not to complain. Draylon and Horse have more family problems than a little bit. The only reason I don't worry about my sister is because I know she can handle herself. Plus, Horse will definitely protect her, so I know she's in good hands.

"Better you than me, dealing with their asses and bread," Horse added.

"What's good, Kei? How is Belladonna coming along? You know Kateevah is dramatic, so she swears her OG isn't healing properly. She wanted her to come and stay with us, but I told her no. That's solely out of respect for you because your wife should be home with you."

"Thanks, bro. I appreciate that. I'm sure Kateevah is worried as fuck. I promise you I'm going to get a handle on that bitch, Myeisha."

"Aye, you're one of my top hitters, so I already know you gone handle that shit accordingly. Don't hesitate to let us know if you need us. We got your back just like you got ours!"

"No question," Horse added.

It felt good to know they had my back the same way I had theirs. Honestly, I've never questioned if they fucked with me like this. It's been like a straight brotherhood since I joined their team. What started as a business has become a big family, and I'm happy to be a part of something so strong and united.

↘ ↘ ↘ ↘ ↘↘

After chilling for a few hours, I headed to the crib. Staying out of the house all day had me beat. Plus, the liquor and the weed had me lifted, so it was imperative I got some fucking sleep. When I stepped into the bedroom, I observed Belladonna sitting on the edge of the bed. She was cleaning her bandages. Seeing the wound on her upper chest made me sad, not to mention mad, because she had no business doing it on her own. It looked like her ass was struggling, too. Leave it to Belladonna to be stubborn and not ask for help.

"You shouldn't be doing that without assistance. Give me a minute. Let me wash my hands, and I'll help you."

"It's cool, Keizon. I got it."

I didn't even answer Belladonna. Instead, I proceeded into our master bedroom and washed my hands. I had a feeling that she was going to piss me off. My goal was not to let her take me out of my element. A nigga was just trying to exercise some patience with her. No matter how I feel about things, I'm already knowing she's feeling much worse.

"Move your hands and let me help." I cleaned the area and applied fresh gauze. It was hard not looking at her big ass titties.

"I'm so fucking glad it's healing good."

"Does it still hurt a lot?"

"Only when I'm laying low. That's why I'm always propped up on the pillows. It's the only way that I can get some sleep. Other than that, I'm good. Nothing for you to worry about."

"What the fuck is that supposed to mean?" That last statement angered me. Why wouldn't I have to be worried about her?

"Huh? What are you talking about?"

"I'm talking about you saying nothing for me to worry about. That sounded fuck up, and it was a fucked-up thing to say. As a matter of fact, you've been real fucked-up to a nigga lately. I've fallen back out of respect for what the fuck you've been through but do me a favor and stop blaming me for what happened. I already feel fucked up about not being able to protect you."

"Keizon, I didn't mean it like that!"

"Yes, the fuck you did! Stop fucking playing in my face, Belladonna!" I didn't mean to yell in her face, but my emotions got the best of me.

"Okay, Keizon! Stop yelling at me! I really didn't mean it like that!" Belladonna started crying and rushed into the bathroom.

I instantly started feeling like shit for losing my cool. It was honestly the last thing I wanted to do, but that comment she made angered the fuck out of me. Belladonna knows how I am about her. It didn't feel good at all making me feel like a fucked-up husband. Maybe I was reaching, but that's how the fuck I felt.

"Why the fuck is you up there doing all of that hollering?" La-La was sitting out on the patio smoking a cigarette. I honestly forgot she was here at the house.

"Stay out of it, Ma!"

She moved closer to me and spoke in a hushed tone.

"I am going to stay out of it. However, I will tell you how I feel. You can't stay away from your wife all day long and then come in and expect her to receive you with open arms. Belladonna knows that you're avoiding her, which makes her feel fucked-up. It's bad enough she's fucked up mentally from being shot. The fact that some deranged bitch did it because of you makes the shit even harder for her. Now I know she and I have had our differences in the past. However, I'm a woman before I'm anything, so I can just imagine how you feel. Calm down and go talk to her."

"Since when have you become so wise?" I laughed.

"Don't make me slap the fuck out of you, Keizon. Listen to what I'm telling you."

"I hear you, Ma. Let me chill out here for a minute, and I'll go up there and apologize shortly."

My phone started going off, so I took it out of my pocket. It was a text from the private investigator.

Magnum PI: *Here is the information you requested. I've added addresses and pictures as well. Thanks for the payment. Let me know if you need any more assistance.*

I didn't hesitate to open the attachments. The first thing I looked at was the pictures and videos. My heart kind of dropped looking at videos of her and a little girl. It was footage of Myeisha dropping her off at school and picking her up. There were many pictures of Myeisha and the little girl. The fact that she wasn't lying about a daughter had me thinking if she could be mine. There is no way this kid could be mine. After scrolling through the videos and pictures, I saved the addresses to my phone. For some reason, I found myself staring at the photos of the little girl. She was, without a doubt, beautiful. Far too beautiful to come from a crazy bitch like Myeisha.

"Is that her daughter?" Hearing Belladonna's voice made me jump.

"Yeah, the private investigator found her info for me."

"Let me see." Belladonna came and sat next to me, and I handed her the phone. She sat quietly as she scrolled through the information. I couldn't tell what she was thinking because her face showed no emotions.

"Don't worry, baby. In the morning, I'm going to handle that bitch. I promise you that."

"What do you mean by handle?"

"You know exactly what I mean? That bitch Myeisha has to pay for shooting you."

"As much as I want her dead for shooting me. It won't feel good knowing we're the cause of a little girl growing up like an orphan. She's innocent in all of this. She shouldn't have to suffer because her mother made a stupid ass decision. Let's just turn her in to the police so that she can get the help she needs." Belladonna handed me her phone and left me on the patio, speechless.

I couldn't believe that she was actually saying this shit. Belladonna is the type of woman who has a heart and a soul. That bitch, Myeisha, doesn't have that. If she did, she would have thought of her daughter before pulling that trigger. From the moment all of this happened, I've been hellbent on murking the bitch, but now Belladonna is switching shit up. I'm more fucked up in the head than I was before.

At first, I wasn't going to say anything about Belladonna's request. However, I have to see if she really wants to handle it like that. Before heading back upstairs, I rolled up a blunt. Belladonna had sobered me the fuck up, not to mention threw me for a fucking loop talking about letting her make it and call the police.

About ten minutes later, I was walking inside the room. She was sitting up in bed with her eyes closed.

"Belladonna! We need to talk about what you're asking." I flamed up the blunt and climbed into bed next to her.

"There really isn't anything to talk about. I just don't want to be the reason that baby grows up without her mom."

"You do know that if Myeisha gets locked up, her daughter is still going to end up living without her, right? She will lose custody, and there is still a good chance she'll end up in foster care. It is a lose-lose situation, baby. Plus, you know I'm not that nigga that allows the police to handle shit for me."

"Well, I don't know what else to say. Just leave it alone for now, but promise me, you won't do anything to her."

All I could do was shake my head, listening to Belladonna. I could not believe she really didn't want me to kill Myeisha's crazy ass.

"I'm only promising to stand down because you want me to. I'm telling you now, I have to keep eyes on the crazy bitch. I cannot allow her to pull another stunt. We could have lost you and never knew what happened. Baby, I can't put your life in limbo. Kateevah will never forgive me if that bitch gets access to you again. Had I never fucked with the bitch in the first place, we wouldn't even be having this conversation. I'll respect your wishes for now, but I really think you need to go ahead and let me murk her."

"Listen to me, Keizon. I'm sorry if I'm doing something unorthodox in your line of work. However, that little girl could possibly be your daughter. What the fuck you gone do? Rush in the house, with guns blazing, while that baby is in the house. Let me guess, you're gone kill her and have that baby expecting her momma to come home, yet she never does? Trust me. Sitting at home waiting for a mother to show up does not feel good."

"I kill niggas all the time and leave they kids orphans. It's not personal. The shit is business, just like this situation is. Kids sometimes have to suffer for the sins of their parents. That's just the way it is. That's not my fucking daughter, so I don't give a fuck."

"I'm not sure if it's denial or delusion. Look at that little girl's picture. She looks like La-La. Do you see that small beauty mark on her cheek? It's the same one you, Tasia, and La-La have. How about you get a DNA test first? I know you think things will change between us if it's your daughter. I promise you it won't. Clearly, she was conceived before we decided to try the relationship thing. You have my word that I'll support you in the event the test comes back positive. I love you, Keizon."

"I love you too. I'm sorry all of this happened."

"You have no reason to be sorry for something out of your control. You've been nothing short of amazing as a husband. There is nothing in this world I'll do when it comes to you. I always give you the benefit of the doubt. I'm sorry for being upset with you."

"You good. I have to think about this whole paternity thing. I'm not feeling it. Out of respect for you, I'll do it. I'm telling you now, if that bitch Myeisha plays any type of games, I'm murking her ass." I placed a kiss on Belladonna's lips and got under the cover with her.

I swear to God. I don't see any resemblance to me in that little girl. I'm lowkey feeling like Belladonna wants her to be mine. The shit feels weird, but I'm going to go ahead and touch basis with Myeisha. She has no clue that I know she shot my wife, so when I pull up on her, she'll be more than willing to do a test.

Chapter 13: Belladonna

After weeks of healing up, I'm feeling the best I've felt mentally and physically. I am so ready to get back to the salon and to my clients. Kateevah and Keizon are the only reason I haven't allowed anyone to start booking again. They are dead set against me going back to work so soon. Speaking of Keizon. I'm sure he's pretty mad at me for asking him not to kill that crazy bitch. However, I don't think I'd be able to live with myself if he did that and never knew the little girl's paternity.

The night I walked onto the patio to apologize to him, observing him staring at the pictures and videos made me want to know, especially after I got a good look at the little girl. That is my husband's daughter. I feel like somewhere inside of him, he knows it's a possibility but is in denial. Keizon can't face the fact that I got shot because of him. Of course, it wasn't his fault per se.

Niggas need to be careful who they fuck around with. Females have feelings, too. It doesn't matter if they're crazy or not. The fact of the matter is he had sex with her, not to mention had her smuggling drugs inside of the prison for him. Amid all of that, she fell in love with him. Now, he must deal with the repercussions of his actions.

Initially, I was so mad at that bitch for shooting me. Don't get me wrong. I still am. It's just that, as a woman, I get how she is scorned. I wouldn't go to those lengths, but in a way, I understand. The paternity test isn't the only reason I don't want Keizon to kill Myeisha. The other reason is that I have my own plan of confronting her. When I had his phone on the patio, I sent the attachments to my phone. Once I saw her address was on there, I didn't hesitate to copy the information. Keizon was so busy trying not to make eye contact that he never saw what I was doing. I have my own plan in motion.

Outside of dealing with this, I've been trying to be patient with my mother being under my roof. It was weird as fuck that she had been acting like the doting mother. When I was in pain and healing, I didn't put up a fight about her staying and helping me out. Honestly, I appreciated how she took care of me. However,

I don't feel like it's genuine. Something inside of me is saying that she has an ulterior motive. Her ass had also got way too comfortable in my guest house. It looks like she didn't book a return flight, which is a problem for me because she can't live here on a permanent basis.

"Good morning. You're looking good," my mother said as she walked into the kitchen where I was sitting.

"Thank you. Can I talk to you for a minute?"

"Sure."

I observed her face distorted a little as she poured herself some coffee. *Yeah, her body language shifted the fuck out of my energy.*

"What are you doing here in Chicago? Before I got shot, you texted and said you would be in town for the weekend. I never responded, but you showed up anyway. Please tell the truth." I was direct and stern while I spoke. Fuck the pleasant tone and all that other bullshit.

"I came because I'm broke and have nowhere to go."

"Didn't you just get married to some rich man?"

I couldn't believe what I was hearing. If my mother didn't do shit else, she collected alimony from every failed marriage. She also received her first husband's pension checks. *How in the fuck could she be broke?*

"That rich man turned out to be a con man. He cleaned me out and stole everything from my accounts." She shed some tears, and I handed her a napkin.

"You are too old to be getting conned out of your fucking money. If you stop going around looking for men to marry, you wouldn't be in this predicament. I cannot believe you. Let me ask you something. Are you expecting me to take care of you? If memory serves me right, you turned your back on me when I needed you. If I were an evil and bitter person, I would do the same to you, but I won't. There are no free rides around here. My husband and I work too hard for what we have."

"I'm not asking you for a free ride, Belladonna. Honestly, I hadn't planned on staying and being a burden on you. However, when I got here and found out you were hurt. I didn't want to leave your side. I understand how you feel about me. You have every right to feel the way you do. I've been off living my own life, yet being around you, Kateevah, and Unique made me realize what I've been missing out on. I'll leave your home, but my goal is to stay here in Chicago."

"I can't force you to leave Chicago. Honestly, it's good to know that you want to be in our life, but I'm not expecting you to stick to that. The first man that comes along, you're going to disappear. Maybe I'm wrong. However, I'm not expecting to see a change with you. I don't care how you do me. Don't come and build bonds with Kateevah and my grandbaby only to turn around and break that bond. Since you have plans on staying, you can live in the apartment that's over the salon. It's fully furnished. Also, your ass gone come out of retirement and start back doing some wash and sets for the seniors."

"I like living in the guest house."

"Well, get used to not living there. Both you and La-La are getting out of my house. Keizon and I like to walk around naked, and we can't do that with y'all walking around in our way. We're cool, but you can't stay here. I got to go. I'm meeting Kateevah for lunch."

"Thanks, Belladonna. I really do appreciate it."

We exchanged hugs, and I headed out before Keizon could catch me. He didn't want me going out of the house without him. I needed to get some much-needed air that didn't consist of him hovering all over me. Don't get me wrong, I love my nigga, but I need some me time.

↘ ↘ ↘ ↘ ↘↘

RBS Brunch and Cafe

"These mimosas are so damn good. Either that or I'm drunk," La-La slurred.

I knew I shouldn't have invited this lush. I'm positive her ass has had at least four mimosas.

"They are good," Kateevah added.

"I'm about to order some more." Tasia gestured to our server.

"Thank y'all for coming out and having brunch with me. It feels so good to be out of the house and feeling better."

We were all sitting around this hot new brunch spot, getting drunk and eating good as fuck. While this invite was very much genuine, I really wanted them to have brunch with me so I could talk to them about the Myeisha situation.

"I'm so happy you're feeling better, Ma."

"That's right, daughter-in-law," La-La slurred. Kateevah and Tasia fell out laughing, and I didn't see shit funny.

"Stop calling me that. Listen, I need to talk to y'all about something."

"Is everything okay?" Kateevah asked, concerned.

"Yes, everything is fine. I want to show y'all something. This is the girl that shot me. The little girl in the picture is supposedly Keizon's daughter. I need y'all help in confronting her."

The table fell silent as they all took turns looking at the pictures. I took that as an opportunity to pour myself another drink.

"Does Keizon know that you have this, Ma?"

"He showed this to me, but he doesn't know I forwarded it to my phone. I want to confront her."

"I'm all for confronting the bitch, but I think you should let Keizon handle this. Plus, there is no guarantee that the kid could be his. There is no telling how many inmates Myeisha was fucking," Tasia added.

"Wait a minute! You know her?" Kateevah questioned.

"I had to meet her before to pick up Keizon's money. That's it."

"What do you think, La-La?" I asked her drunk ass. Before responding, she poured herself another mimosa.

"I think Keizon is going to lose his mind. Belladonna, he is not going to like you going behind his back. This bitch is crazy. There ain't no telling if she'll try to shoot you again. I'm not feeling you going to confront her."

"I'm not going by myself. I want y'all to go with me."

"Draylon will go ballistic if I do that!" Kateevah's ole scary ass was damn near whining.

"Horse will talk so much shit!"

I rolled my eyes, listening to all three of them. It's a damn shame neither of them straight off the back said let's do it.

"Now that we know our niggas will be mad, are y'all going to go with me or not? Look, I feel like it's my responsibility to go and check that bitch. I swear I'm not going to kill her or anything like that. I just want to talk to her," I stressed.

Honestly, I didn't know what the fuck was going to happen. All I know is that I don't want Keizon to just off the back handle shit for me. That crazy bitch needs to know I'm at her ass.

"I'll go with you only if you say you are my daughter-in-law. I'm starting to feel some type of way about you not standing up in your truths."

"Okay, La-La! Damn! I'm your daughter-in-law." La-La jumped out of her seat and ran around to where I was, and she started hugging all over me. We were all laughing at her crazy ass.

"Okay, La-La is in. What about you two?"

"I remember a time when you always fussed at me. What were the words you used to say to me? Oh yeah, I remember, '*Tasia, your ass is always in some bullshit!*' Now look at you involving me in some bullshit. I never thought I would see the day. Can you believe this shit, Kateevah?" Tasia thought she was so fucking funny.

"No. I can't believe it. I'll go with you, Ma, but I'm telling you now, if we get caught, I'm throwing you under the bus."

I couldn't believe Kateevah's scary ass would rat me out.

"I'm definitely throwing her ass under the bus. I'm all in, though. It's been a minute since I've been in some bullshit, so this should be fun."

"This is all fun and games to y'all. I'm going to get my grandbaby out of that crazy bitch clutches. I'm not trying to be funny, Belladonna, but that little girl looks just like me at her age. Plus, she has the same mole as we all do."

"It's cool, La-La. I told him the same thing. Hurry up. We're going to see her now." Initially, I was going to wait until another day, but the way our husbands are set up, we might not get another day when we'll all be able to get out like this.

"Wait! We're going now, Ma?"

"Yes. Let's get the shit over with. We might as well do it now when we're all together." I gave their asses a slick grin and drank the last of my mimosa.

"I have a feeling your ass gone have us in jail," La-La slurred.

"We are not going to jail. Now, let's drink some water so we can sober up."

My phone started ringing, and it was Keizon. Of course, I ignored his ass. I'm not about to answer and give him a chance to fuck up my plan. I'll deal with the repercussions later.

↘ ↘ ↘ ↘ ↘↘

River North

"I can't believe we came out here with no plan. How do you know if that lady is even there?" Kateevah complained.

"Just chill. We're going to wait for about an hour and see if Myeisha comes out or goes in."

"This is a nice area the psycho lives in, too," La-La stated.

"Knowing that bitch she's probably out here hustling niggas for they bread," Tasia added.

We continued to sit and wait until we saw a police car pull up to the building.

"What the fuck?" Tasia yelled.

"Shhh, before they hear us!" I gritted.

"They're about to kidnap her just like they did me," Kateevah said.

We all sat quietly, watching Horse and Draylon step out of the squad car. These niggas were dressed like real fucking Chicago police officers. This shit was crazy.

"My man looks good in that uniform!" Tasia squealed.

"Oh, please! That uniform is tight as hell on Horse," La-La teased. They were laughing, and I was stuck. If they were here doing this, that means Keizon's ass lied to me.

"Let's just pull off before they come back out," Kateevah whined.

I loved my child, but I have to remember to never bring her ass on a caper.

"We can pull off the moment they come back out of the house. I just want to see if they come out with her. For all we know, she might not even be in there."

We all just sat in the car waiting. It seemed like they were taking forever to come back out. Finally, after waiting for about ten minutes, Draylon and Horse emerged from the building. Draylon was holding onto a handcuffed Myeisha while Horse was carrying her daughter.

"What the fuck are they going to do with them?" I questioned.

"They're about to put her ass up somewhere. I'm telling you. This is just like how Draya and Horse kidnapped me. They took me to that big ass mansion and held me into Draylon showed up." I didn't like hearing that.

"Let's just go." I waited until they pulled off and turned down the street before pulling off.

"I don't think Keizon is about to put that bitch up in no mansion. If anything, they might be snatching her ass up to hold her until the paternity test comes back," Tasia stated.

"Yep. I agree. Don't worry, Ma," Kateevah added. I looked in the rearview mirror and looked at La-La's ass, drunk and asleep. Thank God Horse and Draylon got to Myeisha before we did. Her ass would probably have us all locked the hell up.

↘ ↘ ↘ ↘ ↘↘

After dropping everybody back off at their cars, I headed home. The whole time, I wondered exactly what Keizon had planned. I was now lowkey wishing I had just let him move the way he wanted to. Had I done that, he wouldn't have gone behind my back and had them snatched up. Keizon, Horse, and Draylon were all sitting in the living room when I walked inside the house. They were smoking and drinking. If I hadn't just seen these three sneaky motherfuckers with my own eyes, I would think that they had been here the whole time. *How in the fuck did they make it back here before me?*

"What's up, baby? Did y'all enjoy brunch?" Keizon jumped from the couch and started kissing and squeezing on my titties.

"Yeah, we had a nice time. All of those mimosas got me tipsy as hell. I'm about to go shower and lie down for a while.

"I'll be up there in a minute." I rolled my eyes and walked off.

Keizon, Horse, and Draylon were currently playing in my damn face. They asses know we were at that bitch house and saw them. I'm not going to lie. This shit was kind of funny. Them niggas really think they're slick. As I headed up the stairs, I sent Kateevah and Tasia a text about their crazy ass husbands.

All the mimosas I drank were really starting to kick in. Taking a nice hot shower would help sober me up. I'm almost positive Keizon's ass is about to come up here and go off, but I'm going to just take it on the chin because I should have just fallen back and let him handle it.

After a long, hot shower, I dried off and wrapped myself in a towel. When I walked back into the bedroom, Keizon was lying in bed, asshole naked. I was even more confused than before. My pussy got instantly wet watching him jack his dick.

"Come ride this dick, Belladonna."

Keizon didn't have to repeat himself. I dropped that towel and damn near fell, trying to get over to the bed. After all, it had been a minute since we fucked. The moment I slid down on the dick, he started roughly bouncing me up and down.

"Keizon!"

"You've been a bad girl, huh?"

"No! No! I haven't!" I had to grip the sheets to keep from screaming out. He was slapping me hard as fuck on my ass. My cheeks were burning like a motherfucker.

Keizon was fucking me so roughly that he had my fucking chest hurting. I was trying my best to hang out with him, but that was impossible the way he was drilling me. For the first time ever, I felt like I had no business being with this young, big dick nigga. Once he came and he basically lifted my ass up and threw me on the other side of the bed.

"What the fuck, Keizon? Did you forget about my chest?"

"Did you forget about it when your ass was at Myeshia's spot!"

"Huh?"

"Huh, my ass, Belladonna! Did you really think I didn't know you sent that shit to your phone? I was ten steps ahead of your ass from the jump. The only way you wouldn't want me to do something is if your slick ass had something up your sleeve. Thank God I've had Moe following you and the rest of the crew. I'm not mad, baby. I understand. Just tell me what you were going to do?"

"Honestly, I have no idea. I just wanted to confront Myeisha about shooting me and question her about whether you're really the father of her daughter. I'm sorry I went behind your back."

"It's cool. The shit kind of turned me on. That's why I couldn't wait for you to come home so that I could fuck the shit out of you."

"Whatever, Keizon. Your nose is not all the way clean, either. Why would you send Draylon and Horse to snatch them up?"

"Baby, I was just respecting your wishes. You told me to turn her in to the police, so that's what I did. Don't worry about it. Trust me. We haven't killed her, and Kierra is in good hands. When the paternity test comes back, we will decide how to move forward." He grabbed me around the waist and pulled me close.

It felt so good to be in my husband's embrace. I know Kierra is more than likely his, so that means he will more than likely have to raise her. I'm his wife and have no qualms about helping him with that. I guess only time will tell. In the meantime, I just have to fall back and wait for the results to come back.

Chapter 14: Draylon

Things had been running smoothly for me. Every faction that I had reached out to had agreed to fuck with me. Members of the original Council had been talking badly about me, but the shit didn't work because I'm a good ass businessman. Niggas across the city are really fucking with me. The best part of it all is that I've received blessings from our newly elected mayor and the police commissioner. Apparently, they loved the fact that my wife whooped Javanna's ass. Coincidently, she had been extorting them for years. Yeah, that bitch is definitely on borrowed time. I'm surprised I haven't heard from that crazy bitch. I know she is somewhere plotting, but I'm ten steps ahead of her ass.

I had grown impatient, still not knowing who the fuck tried to kill me and my brother. With me having all these business meetings, I had honestly put that shit to the side. However, it's still been heavy on my mind, which has had me thinking. I'm a real street nigga. If that hit had come from an outside force, more attempts would have been made on my life by now. It's been months, and I've been back in the city, moving around freely like a motherfucker. Yeah, that shit came from somewhere closer than I thought. All I have to do is keep thinking and digging deep, and I'll figure it the fuck out.

"The commissioner will see you now, Mr. Prince. Follow me."

I followed behind the secretary, trying my best not to look at her ass. The old Draylon would be nailing her ass to the cross by tonight, but I'm a married man now, so I have to keep that dog in retirement. Kateevah would want to fight if she knew I was looking.

"Come on in, Draylon. I'm sorry I kept you waiting. I had to take an important call. Thanks for coming in at such a short notice. This just couldn't wait until Monday." We shook hands, and I took a seat.

"It's cool. Your message sounded urgent, so I came right away. Did you receive the payment?"

"Yes. This isn't about the payment. It's about your grandmother." I quickly sat up in the seat, hearing him say that.

"What about her?" I bit the inside of my jaw to try to keep calm. If this man was going to tell me she was going behind my back to keep me from getting him on my team, I was definitely going to kill her.

"She put a hit out on you. One of my informants from back in the day reached out to me. He said that he had done hits for your grandparents back in the day. He has since retired from that life. However, he keeps me in the loop about things like this just in case I want in on it. Apparently, she tried to have you killed before, which was the explosion, but you escaped that hit. Your brother wasn't supposed to be in the building that day, which was why she reached out to someone who she knew could get it done properly. She's waiting for him to get back to her. I have him holding off making a move. He has no idea that I'm currently doing business with you."

I sat for a minute, taking in everything the commissioner was saying. My insides churned, and my chest hurt with pain. I'm not going to even lie. My feelings were hurt like a motherfucker. This isn't even about Granny trying to have me killed. It's about wondering what the fuck did I ever do to these people. I blame myself, though. I should have killed her when she sided with my father and sister.

"Good looking. Reach out to your people and let them know they services won't be needed. I'll be in touch with you. Thank you for reaching out to me. I appreciate it."

"Don't mention it. Out of all the people from the streets I've done business with you are by far the most humble and honorable I've ever fucked with. Trust and believe me, the new and improved Prince family has my full support." We shook hands, and I quickly left.

On the ride home, I battled whether or not I should tell Horse. There is really nothing I keep from my little brother. Sometimes, I wish I had never told him about me murking Draya and our pops. It fucked with him for a minute. He was hurt because he loved them but was cool with it because they hurt me. That's a different type of pain feel for a person. I can't put that on him again. He's so focused on opening his business. My little brother needs his head in the game for the shit he's trying to do for himself. I love how dedicated he is to the Prince family. However, he needs to pour into himself and the family he has created. It's better if I don't tell him about this shit with Granny. During the entire drive, I tried to contain my emotions. I was angry and sad. A nigga was sad to the point where I was damn near shedding tears. When I looked in my rearview mirror. I remembered who the fuck I was. It's just fucked up that I have to take drastic measures to remind motherfuckers.

ꓤ ꓤ ꓤ ꓤ ꓤꓤ

"Draylon, it's late baby. When are you coming to bed?"

"I'll be up there in a minute." I turned the Don Julio bottle up and took a long swallow. I thought I had my emotions in check earlier, but I didn't. A nigga fucked around and got lost in a bottle. This old bitch really tried to kill me. I think I'm more fucked up because I didn't kill that bitch sooner. Granny is around my kids on a daily basis. Who's to say that she hasn't been trying to poison them or some shit?

"Nah, you're coming to bed now. Give me this bottle."

"Move, Kateevah!"

"Don't push me like that! What the fuck is wrong with you?" I didn't even realize she slapped the fuck out of me until I started to feel the tingling in my cheek.

"I'm sorry, baby." I quickly dropped the bottle and fell back onto the couch. All I could do was put my head down and shed real nigga tears.

"What's wrong, Draylon? Why are you crying? Say something to me!" Kateevah was pushing my head back, trying to look in my face.

The last thing I wanted was for my wife to see me crying. That shit didn't look right. I was supposed to be stronger than this shit. How in the fuck can she feel protected if I'm crying like a bitch?

"Promise me you won't ever kill me. Leave me first! Do you hear me, Kateevah?" I held her face in the palm of my hands and squeezed a little. Tears were streaming freely down my face as I stared into her eyes.

"I would never do that! I love you, Draylon! Please stop crying! Tell me what's wrong!" Kateevah was on her knees in front of me. One would think I was her fucking son and not her husband by the way she was cradling me. Once I gathered myself. I wiped my face and told her what had me so fucked up.

"Granny is the one who tried to have me killed in the explosion. Horse wasn't supposed to be in the building. She only wanted me dead. The bitch is so evil she's trying to have me killed as we speak. Am I that bad of a grandson that she would try to take me out? Why don't these motherfuckers love me? What the fuck did I ever do to them? I didn't ask to be a part of this shit. It was forced upon me! Am I that fucking expendable that she could just pay someone to take me out?"

"Shhhh! You're going to wake the kids up. Listen to me, Draylon. Baby, this is not about you being a bad grandson. You are a wonderful son, grandson, husband, brother, and father. No one in the world holds this family down like you. The problem is that you're a leader, and you don't march to anyone's beat. You made a conscious step to go your own way, and that bitch doesn't like it. She has never been for you. You and Horse are nothing but pawns in her old ass game. Wipe your face and stand the fuck up. There is no need to be crying. It's time for you to stand the fuck up and do what needs to be done. Anything and anyone trying to take you out needs to be handled accordingly. I love you, and I'll never go against you. Draylon Prince, you are about to be crowned king, so I suggest you straighten your crown and act like it. Come on, let's go upstairs."

"Is Daddy okay?" Hearing Unique's voice made me straighten up. When I looked up, I saw both her and DJ standing not too far from us.

"Yes, he's fine. Just a little sick. Go back to bed." Kateevah rushed over to where they were and ushered them out of the living room.

I needed to get myself together. My kids definitely don't need to see me down like this. In their eyes, I'm a hero, which makes me feel good as fuck. Once I gathered myself, I decided to go and lay it down. Tomorrow was another day, and I planned on handling this shit the right way.

When I reached the top of the stairs, my son was standing there. The little nigga had a look that kind of scared the fuck of me.

"I'm good, son. You can go lay down."

"I won't ever hurt you, Daddy! I'll always protect you just like Aunt Draya taught me."

"I know you will, son. Give me a dap." We dapped it up, and I walked him back to his room. I'm not going to even front. DJ be scaring the fuck out of me. At the same time, I know he's going to grow up and be a fucking beast.

After making sure DJ went back to bed, I headed down the hall to the master bedroom. I stopped in my tracks, seeing Draya standing at the end of the hall. I closed my eyes tight before opening them back up. She was no longer standing there. From time to time, I see her. I'm not sure if it's her ghost or if my mind is playing tricks on me.

I didn't even bother to take off my clothes. The room was starting to spin, and all I wanted to do was sleep this fucking liquor off.

"I have to kill her, Kateevah," I stated with my eyes closed.

"I know, baby, and it's okay. Don't worry, Draylon. I'm going to hold you down to the fullest."

Kateevah wrapped her arm around me and laid on my chest. Her touch alone relaxed me. I don't know where I would be if I didn't have her. I've always felt like I was her safe haven and safe space, which I am. However, I realize that she's the same for me. Every time some shit happens with my fucked-up family, she's right there to hold my hand and speak life into me. It unlocks a different level of our love story. I become more and more obsessed with my wife as time goes by.

*****

The following morning, I was up bright and early, headed to talk to my mother. I'm positive she had no idea that Granny was trying to kill me. Annalise was sneaky, but she wouldn't hurt me or my brother. Now Draya was a different fucking story.

"Good morning, son! What are you doing here?" my mother asked the moment she opened the door for me.

"I needed to talk to you about something."

"Let's go in the kitchen. I just cooked breakfast. Horse was supposed to come to eat breakfast with me this morning, but Junior is sick."

I wanted to decline, but I needed to put something on my stomach. My ass was still drunk from drinking all that fucking Don Julio.

"Talk to me while I warm up your plate."

"I found out who was behind the bombing at Prince Properties."

"Finally. Who sent that hit?" She stopped fixing the plate and gave me her undivided attention."

"It was Granny." Her facial expression dropped the moment the words left my mouth.

"No! Absolutely not. Your grandmother would never do that!" Annalise protested, shaking her head no. I could tell that she wholeheartedly didn't think it was true.

"Well, she did. I got the information from a good source. Not only did I learn she was behind the fucking bombing, but I also learned that she is trying to have me killed as we speak."

"Oh my god, I have to sit down! My blood pressure just skyrocketed. Granny's on her way over here as we speak. She wants me to sign some paperwork for her."

"That's good. I'm going to go outside and pull my car into the garage so that when she pulls up, she won't know I'm here. Call her and see what her ETA is."

"What are you going to do, Draylon?"

"What do you think, Ma?"

"Are you absolutely sure? Maybe your source has it mixed up or something."

"He doesn't have shit mixed up. That old bitch tried to kill me and almost killed Horse. I have her around my wife and my kids. For all I know, she has someone trying to murder them, too. I'm not about to keep letting motherfuckers make it! You're either with me or against me. I'm your motherfucking son! If I say that bitch is trying to have me killed, that's what the fuck it is. You riding or what?"

"I'll always ride for you, son. Go ahead and put the car up. I'll get dressed and call her."

"Try to act as normal as possible. We don't want Granny getting suspicious. Get you a shot or something to calm down. You're shaking." I grabbed my mom by the shoulders, and she relaxed a little.

"I'm shaking because I'm angry, but I'll be okay. I don't need a shot. I've been clean and sober. I can't let anything send me backward. I'm good, son." Annalise kissed me on the cheek and rushed out of the kitchen.

I rushed outside and quickly pulled my car into the garage. I turned my phone off so I wouldn't get any calls before reentering the house. I'm sure at any moment, Kateevah was going to be blowing me up. I slipped out of bed while she and the kids were still sleeping, so a nigga knew I was going to hear her mouth about doing that.

"Granny says she should be here in like twenty minutes. I'm not going to lie, Draylon. I feel like a fucked-up mother right about now. Had I known things would be like this, I would never have gotten with your father. I knew from the jump that he and his family were treacherous. Never in a million years did I think they would hurt you."

"Stop crying. You can't be showing your emotions in Granny's presence. She's not going to even know I'm here. I'll be hiding in the pantry. Let her discuss the paperwork she wants you to sign. That way, she's comfortable."

"Okay. I got you." Annalise wiped her face and drank some water in an effort to calm down.

We spent the next fifteen minutes waiting for Granny to pull up. When she arrived, I quickly rushed into the pantry and listened closely.

"Annalise! Where are you?"

"I'm in the kitchen, Granny!"

"You sure got it smelling good in here."

"I can warm you up a plate. Horse was supposed to come over, but Junior wasn't feeling too good. Is that the paperwork you want me to sign?"

"Yeah, it is. I didn't just come over here for you to sign some paperwork. I need you to talk to Draylon."

"Talk to him about what, Granny? I told you before I'm not getting his business anymore. I think you should just stay in retirement and allow him to move forward with his own faction!"

"If my son were alive, he would support me and make his ass stand down. I have been nothing but nice to Draylon, so for him to try to dismantle everything my husband built and make it his own is disrespectful and ungrateful!"

"Oh please, Granny! If your son were alive, he would be running the Prince family organization into the ground! I'm so confused. Why are you behaving like you have an issue with Draylon all of a sudden?"

"Draylon thinks he's bigger than the family. I don't give a fuck who you are. No one is bigger than the family. I tried to fall back and accept him killing my son and granddaughter. However, as the months passed, I realized what he had done was wrong!"

"No, what Drayton and Draya did to this family was wrong. They went against him, and you did too, Granny! He forgave you. Draylon was one hundred percent right for what he did, and you know it. Your own son used you to get over, so don't sit here acting like he was the son of the year because he wasn't, nor was he a good husband or father. Let me sign these papers so you can leave. I'm not really feeling this conversation."

"Well, it's a conversation that needs to be had. My biggest regret is not allowing Horse to be the head of the family. He would never run things the way that Draylon is. I'm going to use my powers to keep Draylon from starting a new faction. I tried talking to him, but he didn't want to hear me out. I even tried to speak with Kateevah, and that fat bitch disrespected me. Now, I'm talking to you, and you're brushing it off. I'll handle Draylon my way."

I had heard enough and was over this bitch talking shit about me. Before stepping out of the pantry, I grabbed a black garbage bag. Granny's back was to the pantry, so she never saw me. In one swift motion, I placed the bag over her head and started smothering the fuck out of her old ass.

"Ahhhh!" she screamed and tried getting out of my grip, but I was too strong for her ass. She was a tough old bitch because she was not going down easy.

My mother grabbed a big-ass butcher knife and started stabbing Granny while I continued to suffocate her with the bag. Moments later, she was no longer moving.

"What the fuck is y'all doing?" Hearing Horse made both me and Annalise freeze in place. I locked eyes with my brother and Tasia. She was holding Junior in her arms.

"Oh my god!" She screamed.

"Take him upstairs, Tasia!" my mother screamed, quickly rushing Tasia out of the kitchen and leaving us alone.

"I'm sorry. I didn't tell you, bro. She left us no choice."

"Draylon, you killed Granny!" Horse blurted, panicking a little.

"Calm down, bro. I found out that she was the one behind the attempt on my life. You weren't supposed to be there. I survived, so she has been trying to get me killed again. The bitch had to go, bro! It was either her or me!" I explained.

"You could have fucking let me know. I didn't want my wife and son seeing that shit."

"I'm sorry, bro. I didn't want to tell you and put that burden on you. Do you really think this shit is easy on me? I've been trying my best not to let it come down to this, but that bitch left me no choice. I've never done shit to her, yet the old bitch been against me from the jump."

"We good, bro. Fuck are we gone do with her body?" Horse yelled.

"Put her in the woodchipper on the Prince Estates! Granny can join her good-for-nothing ass son and granddaughter she spoke so highly of. Let me get cleaned up and take care of my sick grandson. Don't worry about, Tasia. She's one of us. Get that bitch out of my house ASAP!" Annalise interjected before exiting the kitchen and leaving us alone.

"Had I known this shit was going on, I would have put on the clothes I wear to get rid of fucking bodies! Let's get this shit cleaned up, bro. We'll talk about this later. Don't let this shit get to you. I'm already knowing you did what the fuck you had to do. At least now, the new and improved Prince family can start to flourish across the city." We dapped it up and started cleaning up the kitchen.

As we wrapped Granny's body up in an Oriental rug, I felt nothing. At one point, my grandmother was one of my favorite people in the world. How she could try to have me taken out is beyond me. It's cool, though. Now she's in hell with the rest of the motherfuckers who thought it was okay to cross me.

Chapter 15: Horse

It had been hours since we got rid of all the evidence. The kitchen was so fucking clean that it looked like there had never been a fucking bloody crime scene. Here it is I've been thinking I'm the crazy one out of the family, but the whole time it's Draylon and Annalise's asses. They looked like real killers when I walked into the kitchen. I'm pissed Tasia saw that shit. It was a good thing Junior was sleeping. We decided to come over and eat breakfast before taking him to urgent care. I really wish we would have gone straight there. I'm positive Tasia would never speak about what she saw, but at the same time, seeing someone murdered is not easy to deal with. Plus, I don't want her to think that we're so ruthless that we just kill family members.

"Bro, I just want you to know I'm sorry."

"Stop apologizing, bro. You did nothing wrong. I'm sure it doesn't feel right, but you had to do it. Stop beating yourself up and go home. I'm about to take Tasia and Junior home now. Ma broke Junior's fever some kind of way, so now he's feeling better. Always remember it's either them or us, and we're going to choose us every time! I love you, big bro!"

"I love you too." Draylon pulled me in for a brotherly hug, and we dapped it up. He needed to know that I had his back through whatever.

Never in a million years did I think there would be only three of us left. Honestly, I saw us all getting older and wealthier. It was our time to change the Prince family narrative. Out with the old and in with new things. I'm fucked up about Granny, but the bitch had no right to try to kill my brother. To make matters worse, she almost killed me.

Although we're up and walking around, we're still fucked-up physically from that shit and have to have physical therapy to get our strength back. Just when I thought the family could get no worse than my sister and pops, Granny showed us how shit gets even worse. She had long ago turned into a different grandmother than the one who had a hand in raising me.

↘ ↘ ↘ ↘ ↘↘

It was later that night, and I was lying in bed staring at the ceiling. Sleep was not coming easily for Tasia or me. We were both lying in bed, awake, not saying a word.

"Are you okay, Dayvion?" Tasia asked for the hundredth time.

"I'm good. Go to sleep. I know it's been a long day for you."

"Horse, I doubt if I'll be able to sleep for a couple of days. Plus, I'm so worried about you."

"I'm good. I just don't want you to look at my family like we're fucked up. What you saw today was something I never wanted you to see. I want you to know I would never do anything like that to you. All I ask is that you never cross me or make me question your love. That shit would destroy me, Tasia. The way my father, sister, and Granny have been against us has killed a piece of me. That shit doesn't feel good. It's like our childhood was some big ass lie. What the fuck happened to my family, Tasia?"

"First and foremost, I would never do anything to make you feel that way. I love you more than anything in this world. I'll never judge you based on the actions of your family. Clearly, Annalise and Draylon did what they had to do. Hearing she was behind trying to have Draylon killed angered me. You could have died and left us all alone, so killing her was a justified move. Horse, you cannot dwell on what the Prince family used to be. That part of this life no longer exists. It's time for a new and improved Prince family organization. No matter what I saw today. As a matter of fact, what are you talking about? I didn't see anything today."

Tasia straddled me and pulled her panties to the side. My dick is always hard and ready, so I slipped inside of her warm ass pussy. When she pulled her Walmart gown up over her head. I knew she was about to go crazy on the dick. As I gripped her hips, I slowly bounced her up and down on the dick until I was cumming full force inside of her. If her ass weren't still sneaking and taking birth control, I'm sure her ass would be knocked up with my seed. She thinks I don't know, but I do. I'm not mad about it, especially since she's getting ready to embark on this new journey with the supper club. We have plenty of time to have more kids.

About ten minutes later, Tasia was sound asleep. I still

couldn't doze off, so I headed downstairs to grab a bottle of water. A nigga must have been thirsty because I drank the whole thing. When I opened the garbage lid to throw it out. I noticed a letter sitting on top. As I retrieved it from the garbage can, I remembered it was the same letter I told Tasia to throw in the garbage months back. *Why wouldn't she throw it away and then never read it?* Now, I was intrigued. I didn't hesitate to open it and read it. My eyes bucked out of my head, seeing who it was from.

Dear Dayvion,

If you're reading this letter, I am more than likely dead. Don't think too hard about why I sent it without any information. I had an associate I paid to send you this letter in case she never saw me again. I'm sorry I hurt you and Draylon. That was never my intention. Things just spiraled out of control, and I couldn't fix it. Pops had my back against the wall, and you know how intimidating he can be.

Horse, I want you to know that you have always been my best friend and protector. You have been the best big brother a girl like me could have asked for. Honestly, I never deserved the love you and Draylon gave me. The idea of having more power ruined me. I was tired of running things Draylon's way. I didn't appreciate him making us babysit his bitch and their baby. Then you started running up behind her friend. When they came along, I felt like my brothers had forgotten about me. It felt like you and he no longer loved or needed me, so it was easier for me to gravitate toward Pops. That's neither here nor there at this point. I'm sure that my actions have you hating me, too. Just know and understand that you lacked nothing as a friend or a brother. I'm not going to hold you, big bro. I just wanted you to know that I LOVE YOU!

-Draya

I didn't hesitate to tear the letter up. I'm sure Draya's words came from a genuine place. However, her actions showed me who the fuck she really was. I've come to terms with her treachery, so I didn't need this bullshit-ass letter. If there is anything I learned from all of this, it's to believe a person's actions, not what the fuck they say out of their mouths. Fuck her and that fake-ass love. Draya did more than just side with our father. The stunt she pulled with DJ happened years before, so from the jump, she has had treachery in her heart, so yeah, the letter was a bunch of bullshit. I'm glad Draylon got rid of the bad apples of the family. Now we can live the happily ever after we've worked so hard for. I'm ready for a new beginning for the Prince Family.

Chapter 16: Kateevah

"Mommy, can I try to call Granny again?"

"I told you Granny is on vacation handling business. I'm sure she'll call when she gets a chance. How about you call Grandma Belladonna and see if you can come to spend the night with her?"

Unique had been driving me crazy to call Granny. It had been damn near a month since Draylon and Annalise killed her, but my poor baby really wanted to hang out with her partner-in-crime. It's killing me seeing Unique constantly trying to contact Granny, but at the same time, I'm happy that old bitch is dead and gone. I can't believe that she really was trying to take Draylon out. That hurts my heart because he had really been trying not to kill her. Still, in the end, Granny left him no choice. I'm just as happy as hell that he learned before it was too late.

I've watched him day in and day out like a hawk. On the one hand, I'm worried about him. On the other hand, I know that my husband will be just fine. I can only imagine how he must feel on a daily basis knowing that he had to murder his father, sister, and grandmother. The shit is beyond my understanding. The truth of the matter is that it's not for me to understand. My job is to be the supportive wife that my husband needs. Lord knows Draylon needs me now more than ever. I've got his back and his motherfucking front, so he doesn't have shit to worry about. It's his time to shine, and I'm going to see to it that there are no more threats against us.

With everything that had been going on, I decided to throw a barbecue at the house for everybody. With all the things that had transpired recently, I thought it would be a good idea to get fucked up and eat some ribs.

"Do you need me to help with anything else? If not, I'm about to get in the pool with my grandkids," Annalise spoke as she came into the kitchen, holding the meat she had just taken off the grill.

"I actually do need your help with something."

"What is it?"

"I need you to get me access to that squad car they be using."

"Oh no! Your ass is not about to have me in trouble with

Draylon and Horse. With the way that motherfucker around here offing family members. I'm walking a thin fucking line, Kateevah!"

I couldn't help but fall out laughing. The look on Annalise's face was priceless.

"I'm serious. I need it to handle something."

"Handle what?"

"Do I have to tell you?"

"Hell yeah, you have to tell me so that I can know whether or not you need my help. Kateevah, you are not about that street life, my dear daughter-in-law. Now tell me!" Annalise pressed.

"I need it to see I can get at that lawyer bitch, Javanna. Draylon doesn't know, but I've seen some texts she sent him a couple of days ago. She's still trying to get me locked up, and she wants him to get her pregnant. I'm telling you, she's a sick-ass bitch. Draylon is not in his right state of mind to have to deal with her ass. However, I'm at full mental capacity. Are you going to help me or not?"

"I'll help you get access to it, but I have to go with you. I can wear Draya's old uniform. You should be able to fit the one that Horse be wearing."

I fell out laughing because there was no way she thought I was putting on Horse's police uniform.

"I'm big, but I'm not that damn big. I've already ordered my uniform. I'm sexy as fuck in it, too. I have to look good as fuck when I snatch that bitch up!"

"So, when are we doing this with your crazy ass?"

"We ride at dawn. I found out Javanna's route to work, and she makes it to her office every morning at seven."

"How in the fuck do you know that lady's route to work?"

"Let's just say Draylon is not the only one with connections. Thanks, Annalise."

"You know I got you." She winked at me and went back outside.

As I looked out of the patio door, I observed my momma and Keizon playing in the pool. Horse was trying his best to throw Tasia in the pool, but she was running from him. Draylon and DJ were off to the side, engaged in deep conversation. La-La and Grandma Donna were laid back smoking joints. This is what family is supposed to be about — getting together and having the time of your life. There should never be a time when you can't trust the family you come from or create. The scene before me is something that I pray we continue to see for many years to come. Thank God Draylon got rid of the bad apples. Now I can handle this bitch who wants to cause problems for us.

$$\searrow \searrow \searrow \searrow \searrow\searrow$$

The Next Day

"What's up, Ma? I came right over when you texted me." My mother was sitting in her living room sipping some wine. I quickly grabbed a glass from the bar and poured me some.

"The paternity test came back." She looked a little scared, not to mention nervous. I had to grab her hand to stop her from shaking.

This whole thing has had my momma on pins and needles. I don't see why she is so nervous about the results. From the jump, she has had the expectation that the little girl was indeed Keizon's seed. It was he who didn't believe it.

"What was the result?"

"It was a positive match."

"Where's Keizon? How does he feel about it?"

"I'm not sure. When Keizon opened the results, he walked straight out of the house. I don't know. I'm just nervous that he might do something crazy."

"Don't be sitting here worried about that bitch and what happens to her. She came to your place of business and tried to kill you. She doesn't care about you, Ma. If anything, she hates you because you have something that she can't have. You raised me to have a caring spirit about people, but at the same time, she is none of your concern. Myeisha has to deal with the repercussions of her behavior. If Keizon kills her, then so be it."

"I don't care about her. I've always felt like the results were going to be positive. I'm just concerned about him actually raising a daughter. He knows nothing about it, and I'm too damn old to be starting over. I'm positive he went to get her. I don't know, Kateevah. I guess I'm nervous because bringing a kid into the fold will be different for us. Give me some advice. How did you deal with DJ's presence?"

Before responding, I poured more wine into our glasses.

"At first, it was kind of hard because DJ's little ass is crazy. He kind of scared me, but with patience, I learned to understand that Draya raised him fucked-up. Instead of distancing myself from DJ, I decided to be more hands-on with him. He needed motherly love, and that's what I gave him. You will definitely have to be hands-on with Keizon's daughter. Keizon doesn't know anything about kids. It won't be solely on you, though. I already know La-La and Tasia will have a hand in raising her, too. You have always been a great mom, so there isn't a doubt in my mind that you'll be okay."

"Thanks, daughter. I needed that. Who knew I would be getting advice from you? I swear you've grown up to become such a beautiful woman, wife, and mother. I'm proud of you."

"Awww, thanks, Ma." We gave each other a hug and continued to sip from our wine glasses.

I wanted to let my mom in on what I had planned for that lawyer bitch. However, with her having her own issues she was dealing with, I decided to keep it to myself. Plus, I need to keep it to myself. I couldn't risk anyone messing up what I have planned for that Javanna bitch.

The door opened, and Keizon walked in with the little girl in tow. I gestured for my mom to get up and greet them.

"I had to go get her and bring her home with me, baby. Ain't that right, Kei Baby!" I smiled, looking at the beautiful little girl bend down and tie her shoes.

"Yes, Daddy! That's right. Hi, I'm Kierra! What's your name?"

"I'm Belladonna, and this is my daughter Kateevah."

"Hey, pretty girl. I have a daughter, and her name is Unique. One day soon, I'm going to let you come over to my house and play with her."

"Can I, Daddy?"

"Of course."

"Where is Myeisha?" My mother questioned.

"She lost her head that day the police snatched her up." Keizon stated without batting a fucking eye. I took that as my cue to leave. Keizon had stood on big business behind Belladonna.

"Let me get home. Call me if you all need anything. Congratulations, Keizon. I'm so happy for you. You got this, and you do too, Ma. I love y'all." I tried not to make eye contact with her because I knew her ass was thinking about what he had revealed.

"We love you, too." She spoke. I gave them both a hug and left. They needed time alone to bond with Keirra. I'm glad Keizon killed that bitch. She never should have shot my fucking momma.

*****

"Come in here and sit down." Draylon spoke sternly the moment I walked in the door. Looking at Annalise sitting across from him let me know her ass ratted me out. He had the meanest scowl on his face.

"You ratted me out, huh?"

"I'm sorry, Kateevah. This time around I couldn't indulge in anything like that. If something happened to you. I could never forgive myself. You know his ass would kill me if you got hurt. Please forgive me." Annalise pleaded.

"It's cool. I'm sorry for getting you involved."

"Leave us alone for a minute, Ma!" I was thinking I should probably make a run for it. Then again, let me sit my ass down and get cussed out.

"Before you go off, Draylon! Please hear me out! I just wanted to handle her myself. Plus, I know that you're already going through a lot. Not to mention, you have enough on your plate."

"Let me stop you, right there! No matter what the fuck I got going on. You never go behind my back and try to handle anything."

"But Draylon!"

"Nah! Ain't no motherfucking but, Kateevah! Listen to me and listen to me clearly! This is a conversation that you and I will never have again. So, let me speak and don't say shit back. Are you following me?" He flamed up a blunt and took a long pull.

"Yes Draylon!"

"Since I met you. You've always been one of those women who get wrapped up in them crazy ass Urban Fiction books. I am here to tell you that our love story pans out different as fuck. I'm not like these other niggas. My wife will never tote guns or have bodies under her belt on the account of me. Let me ask you a question. Have you ever murdered someone?"

"No. I haven't."

"Trust and believe me. That shit isn't easy. Niggas kill other niggas every day. Just because they are walking around smiling. Don't mean they aren't affected by it. I am haunted by the ghost of my sister on a daily basis. That shit don't feel good, Kateevah. I would never want that for you but that's what happens when you snatch a life. That person's ghost will haunt the fuck out you. It doesn't matter if you had no other choice. The shit sticks with you every day.

For the record, I'm not mad at you for feeling like you had to step up. I don't need you to do that for me. I am not that husband you read about in them books. I'm that husband that wants you to be a wife and a mother. That's it and that's all. I'll handle the rest. I married you because you were different. I've fucked with street bitches all of my life. They could never rock my last name. You get that privilege because you're a different type of bitch. I mean that in the most respectful way. Don't ever go behind my back and pull no shit like that again! Don't cry, Kateevah. This conversation is not to hurt you. It's to let you know that I will spazz the fuck out. If I ever find out you were on some bullshit like that again. Now go pack."

"Go pack for what!"

"I'm taking the family on vacation. Everybody is packing as we speak. Give me a kiss." Draylon pulled me into his embrace and kissed me deeply.

"I need to know what you're going to do about her. She's not going to just go away. I saw those texts she sent the other day. Do you think going on vacation is okay, right now?"

"Let me show you something. Since you seem to think I'm not capable of handling shit. I wasn't even going to show you this but fuck it."

Draylon pulled his burner phone out and showed me a picture. I instantly felt like I was going to throw up all of the wine I had just drank. It was a picture of the lawyer bitch head.

"Oh my God!"

"Really Kateevah! You're about to throw up looking at a decapitated head! How in the fuck were you going to go and kill her. It's a good thing my OG came clean. Your ass would have probably ending up in jail. I was never going to allow her to get away with anything. The details aren't needed so don't ask no questions. While you were ordering uniforms and shit. I was torturing that bitch and cutting off her fucking head! Nobody fucks with my baby and lives to talk about it. Now go pack you and the kids clothes."

"I love you so much, Draylon. I don't know what I would do without you."

"I love you too and I'll protect you until my dying day."

As I stood in the middle of my living room with my arms wrapped around my husband. While passionately kissing him. I can't help but get lost in our love story. This man had been my knight in gangster armor from the moment he had me snatched up. Despite the bumps in the road and the haters. We overcame it all. I never thought I could find a man to love me and my size. Let alone build a life with me and kill for me. I never knew I was worthy of that type of love. Draylon Prince came into my life and changed all of that. I now truly understand how a gangster can fall in love and become obsessed with a BBW. The shit started with a one night stand and ends with a happily ever after.

This is the end of this series but not the ending of us. We will see you guys again in December. Prepare yourselves for

A Prince Family Christmas!!

THE END

Made in the USA
Columbia, SC
07 September 2024

41961906R00065